"Did you bribe them to play a waltz? What a shocking waste of money. They have been instructed to play several, included in their fee."

His eyes glowed strangely bright. "I think I'm going to kiss you, Clara," he said in a husky voice. "Don't you think we should go somewhere more private?"

"What, and waste your guinea? No, no, like your primitive urges, it will soon pass."

His feet stopped moving. He stood stock-still in the middle of the floor, arousing some curiosity as waltzers jostled around them. "I don't think so. It seems to be getting stronger. If you don't want to scandalize Auntie's party still further, you had best come with me."

WINTER WEDDING

Joan Smith

FAWCETT CREST • NEW YORK

Library of Congress Card Number: 90-90292

ISBN 0-449-21786-8

Manufactured in the United States of America

First Edition: December 1990

Chapter One

There was so much bustling activity going forth under the roof of the Lucker residence, Branelea, that the barren view from the windows was scarcely noticed. December was upon them, laying waste the beauty of the countryside without yet hiding its vandalism under a covering of snow. About the only pleasant sight for miles around was Branelea itself. Its austere beauty was strangely enhanced by the sere grass that shook in the wind and the naked black arms of trees that twitched as if they would clutch at the house for protection.

The house was built in the Perpendicular style with no soaring Gothic windows, no spires or finials, or even a graceful columned doorway. Lady Lucker had a taste for the elegant, and the bleak gray walls of home could well do with a little garniture in her view. But it was Sir James's ancestral home—large, in good repair, free of mortgage, and therefore tolerated.

As Lady Lucker sat in her gold saloon on that chilly morning, it was not her gray walls that occupied her mind. Nor was it the festive season, fast approaching. She had a matter of greater and dearer moment to consider. Her daughter Prissie was to be married at the end of the month.

She sat with a list in front of her, which she was checking over with her houseguest, Miss Christopher. Lady Lucker was no connoisseur of female beauty. She could scarcely have described Clara Christopher, though they spent endless hours together. "A pleasant girl," she would have said, if asked. Chestnut curls, brown eyes, and a figure that caused a second look from men cut no ice with her.

"I have been planning this wedding for three years," she said with a sigh. "Ever since I fell into the expensive folly of giving my elder daughter a London wedding. You wouldn't believe what the hotel charged me for the dinners! Of course I nabbed an earl for Emily, and that was worth any price. Emily's husband was instrumental in getting my elder son a seat in Parliament and a couple of appointments to go along with it and give him some money. Such a take-in, the members not getting paid! I had no idea . . . And of course with Emily having a house in London, Prissie had her season at very little cost. That is when she nabbed your cousin, Baron Oglethorpe, Clara."

"Why did you choose the twenty-ninth of December for the wedding, ma'am?" Miss Christopher asked with an innocent smile in her brown eyes, though she had a sharp idea as to the reason.

"Why to cut short the length of the visits," Lady Lucker answered frankly. "I assume the guests will

2

celebrate Christmas at their own homes, and not be barging in an inconvenient week early. Then you know, it has been a long-standing tradition that Sir James and I spend New Year's in London with Sir James's Uncle Percy, so that the guests cannot hang on too long after the wedding." No blush suffused the lady's face at this plainspeaking. The only little prevarication was that the "long-standing tradition" was instituted in November of that same year.

"Very wise," Miss Christopher said. "And for the few days they are here, I daresay the overflow from the wedding feast will feed them."

"With something left over to take along to Uncle Percy. One dislikes to go empty-handed. Mrs. Horst is making a gigantic wedding cake. I praised the one she made for her own daughter assiduously, till she finally took the hint and offered to have her cook make Prissie's."

Miss Christopher nodded and managed to keep her lips steady. She knew that similar praise of patties, punches, and petits fours had been lavished about the countryside till the feast was as well as on the table without expenditure of a thing but words. Every spare fowl in the parish was being fatted up for the great day, and every egg was requisitioned to be put into a syllabub or pudding. There was enough food coming to feed an army, and an army was what was to assemble at Branelea at the end of the month, to see Miss Priscilla Lucker pledge her troth to Baron Oglethorpe, of Oglethorpe Manor in Hampshire and Hanover Square in London.

"I hope she doesn't stint on currants," Lady

Lucker said, frowning at her list. "I have notified the guests of Prissie's pattern in china and silver plate and crystal. The poor girl hasn't a decent jewel to her name. I do hope her Uncle Max takes the hint. A four-figure income, and he was always so fond of Prissie."

All the relations were imagined to be fond of Prissie. That such an unappealing lump as Prissie had engendered so much fondness was, of course, a sham, like so much in that house. She was a vapid blond lady with no conversation, the unlikeliest daughter in the world for Lady Lucker. The mama was a skint, but such a lively, good-natured one that she had a large circle of friends. Clara liked her very much. Her being clutch-fisted was just an interesting oddity. When one traveled as much as Clara, one met all kinds of people.

"Bachelors and widowers often give jewelry," Clara mentioned. "They mistrust their taste in household things, I suppose."

"The ones who diddle you are the maiden aunts. My own aunt gave Emily monogrammed sheets and pillowcases—to a *countess,* imagine! I let them know that Prissie has all her linen assembled," Lady Lucker said, with a sapient shot from her black eyes. "I suggested perhaps they would find it easier to send money, and Prissie could pick up half-a-dozen place settings of the Wedgwood herself. They would palm the poor girl off with a couple of guineas if I did not give them a little hint of what is expected. As to Sir James's maiden cousins, the Snelley spinsters, they sent Prissie a homemade bed jacket and flannalette

4

nightie. As if a baroness would be caught dead in such things!"

"Shocking!" Miss Christopher tch'd.

"They said they doubted they could attend the wedding, which is as well for them."

An innocent observer might be forgiven for thinking the Luckers were purse-pinched, but Clara Christopher knew it was far from being the case. Sir James was as well inlaid as any gentleman in the parish, but to state it simply, his wife was the premier skint in all of England. She actually enjoyed scrimping and saving. This wedding was a challenge to achieve the maximum of showy elegance with the absolute minimum of expenditure. It was a chore to daunt a less able skinflint than Lady Lucker, but it did not daunt her.

The truth would not dawn on anyone who had not actually resided under the same roof with her for some time. Miss Christopher, a fairly astute observer, had not tumbled to it for two weeks. Of course, special care was taken to conceal it from her, for she was Oglethorpe's cousin. That a mere cousin of a groom-to-be should find temporary shelter with Lady Lucker was an unusual thing in itself. A close relative had difficulty getting through the door unless his visit promised profit to his hostess.

There was, of course, a reason for the visit. Lady Lucker made the quite natural mistake of thinking Oglethorpe's first cousin was rich. There was Charles, the scion of the Lucker family, still without a wife. Miss Christopher, she was given to understand, had excellent connections and a far-flung network of friends as well. Surely some of them had homes in Brighton or Bath. A free holiday was not to be disregarded.

Miss Christopher, now called Clara, was an orphan who had been residing with an aunt who had just married and gone on a honeymoon to Greece. A twenty-two-year-old niece could not but be a hindrance at such a romantic time. Oglethorpe had done no more than mention Clara's predicament and the invitation was extended instantly. He had not quite come up to scratch in offering for Prissie at the time, and really there was no saying the invitation had not clinched it. So in a way Lady Lucker did not regret her openhandedness, even when it was gradually borne in on her that Miss Christopher, far from being rich, hadn't two sous to rub together.

The early weeks of Clara's visit were a period of mutual discovery. Clara had seen enough of half-drunk wine being surreptitiously poured back into decanters and enough of shoddy household fixtures being polished and pinned to appear decent that she had a fair notion how the house was run. A few good pieces of old furniture formed a rich backdrop, but the rest of it was a sham.

Not a stick of furniture could be moved, for if its location did not hide a bare patch of carpet, its scratched side had to be placed against a wall. The Meissen ware that adorned tabletops was never to be touched. If it did not have a pasted-on handle, it was sure to be concealing a burn or scratched surface. You dare not jiggle the chairs for fear of pulling a leg loose, and even the sheets disliked a restless sleeper, so precariously were they held together. Yet to enter the gold saloon, one would think it an excellent chamber. In the two weeks of her visit, Clara had disturbed enough of the surface of things to realize what was going on.

During the same period Lady Lucker had gone into Clara's room when the girl was out walking and seen her lingerie was of well-mended cotton. Her face cream was an inferior brand (the same brand as her own), her combs and brushes were plain bone. Her money, accidentally chanced upon at the bottom of her leather jewelry bag, amounted to no more than a few guineas, and she was to stay two months!

As these mutual revelations were assimilated, the reserve and politeness of the relationship dwindled to comfortable familiarity, unmarred by any taint of condescension. Before the third week was out, Clara was helping to save bits of paper and string and cutting buttons off old shirts for Lady Lucker, and the hostess was directing Clara to the remnant bin at Dunston's Drapery Shop to pick up bits of leftover muslin for a fraction of the cost of buying it by the yard. With careful contriving, at which Clara was a bit of a dab herself, a collar and cuffs or a handkerchief could be pieced together at a nominal cost.

Clara was always relieved when the roles became understood in the houses where she was staying. It was uncomfortable to be treated as a guest when one was the only guest in the house and there for an extended time. Over a long career of visiting, she had acquired a certain ease of manners that usually settled this matter of roles quickly. She liked best to be treated as a member of the family. She usually *was* a member, however tenuous, of the various houses she visited and had a knack of discovering genteel ways of helping without taking on the coloring of a domestic. She was quite firm on that point. At two and twenty, she had no notion of becoming a permanent, unpaid companion to any invalid aunt or anything of that sort.

She had been orphaned ten years before, and though her family connections were numerous and good, her own parents were not well-off. Various relatives had offered her a home, but however much she liked to visit, she was always happy to move on and try her luck elsewhere. She thought of herself as a sort of eternal wandering guest, living out of trunks. Home was the stagecoach, and her backyard was the roads of London and Scotland. She had heard of a plant in America that had no roots but rolled about the countryside, and in a fanciful mood she thought of herself as a human tumbleweed. If she was still single at twenty-five, she planned to find a position, perhaps as a paid companion to some rich female *cit* who liked to travel.

At the present, however, she had no fear of the future, nor any fear that she would not find a husband. She liked men, was perfectly at ease with them, and the liking was reciprocated. She had turned down three offers, which, considering her rootless life and lack of fortune, was not bad. But for the present, she would continue to accept such offers as were made of taking her in as a guest.

She had never stayed in Surrey before. She

thought she would like it in a more benign season than winter; she was happy they had the approaching wedding to relieve the tedium of a restricted company and limited entertainment.

"As we have nothing better to do, Clara, let us begin writing up the place cards for the wedding dinner table," Lady Lucker suggested. "You recall the cards I bought at the stationer's."

"They're in the library." Clara said not a word about the cards being "bought." A dozen had been bought, but there were a hundred guests to be seated. The other eighty-eight cards had been ruled up and cut out of white cardboard by herself.

"I have the list of guests about somewhere. We'll just write up the cards today, and settle on the seating arrangement later."

"The list is in the library with the cards. Shall we do it there?" Clara suggested, happy to have found some genteel occupation.

The ladies were soon settled at the reading table, with the lists, cards, ink pots, and pens before them. "You take this sheet. I'll take the other," Lady Lucker said, handing Clara a sheet of names. That able nip-cheese, Lady Lucker, only used new paper for letters. For such things as lists, she used wrapping paper smoothed with an iron. Her watery ink made the names even more difficult to read. Glancing at the sheet, Clara felt a sudden quiver rush over her scalp. That name looked remarkably like Allingcote. But it couldn't be. No, it did not say *Lord* Allingcote. B. Allingcote, it said.

9

After her heart settled down, Clara asked with a casual air, "Who is this B. Allingcote, ma'am?"

"That is my sister Peg's boy. Lord Allingcote of Braemore. Do you know him?" Lady Lucker showed no surprise. She had already discovered that in spite of Clara's poverty, she was acquainted with everyone and had visited with the half of Scotland and England.

No tide of scarlet washed over Clara's face. Her voice did not tremble as she replied, "I met him once, I believe, at a house party some time ago at the Bellinghams'."

"Very likely. He visits about a good deal. We hoped he would settle down after his papa died and he became the earl, but he persists in his runabout ways. I doubt he will come to the wedding, however. His mama mentioned something about his going to Scotland. He will send a gift, of course. He is fond of Prissie."

"Shall I make him a card, just in case?" Clara asked blandly. Her fluttering heart settled down. In that half a minute, she had envisaged a remeeting, a whirlwind courtship, and a proposal of marriage, but nothing of all this speedy romance showed in either her face or voice.

"No point in wasting a card. Just don't cross out his name on the list."

As they continued their work, Clara's eyes were drawn again and again to that name, that stood out because of the lack of a line through it. Lord Allingcote . . . Dormant memories stirred to life at the back of her mind.

Chapter Two

It had been two years ago that Clara met Allingcote at the Bellinghams' house party, where an amateur production of *The Tempest* was being put on. Allingcote would have met several hundred ladies since then and enjoyed a flirtation with a few dozen of them, as he had with herself at the Bellinghams'. He had particularly complimented her on her new rose taffeta gown, the same one she meant to wear to the wedding, only embellished now with a length of lace around the bodice and sleeves. Skirt ruffles were not for her. Yards and yards of lace they took and were reduced to dusty ribbons in a fortnight. Wouldn't it be horrid if he came and recognized the gown! Wouldn't it be worse if he didn't even recognize *her*! But he was probably not coming at all.

Clara had never once seen Allingcote since the house party at the Bellinghams', but strangely, she kept hearing about him. They seemed to go to many of the same places, unfortunately at different times. Even Scotland, so out-of-the-way and where she had twice visited her aunt, had been on his route. He seemed to be as rootless as herself—worse. He was willfully rootless, for he had a home of his own and traveled apparently from mere caprice.

It seemed she often received a reply to a letter from a recent hostess to hear that Allingcote had been there shortly after she left. These frequent references to him kept him alive in her mind, but she didn't think she would have quite forgotten him in any case. She even suspected that she had been a little in love with him. Much good it would do her! A well-landed earl was not likely to consider an impoverished tumbleweed a suitable bride.

Lady Lucker rattled on to say that Allingcote had developed quite an interest in Scotland lately. He had paternal relatives there. The name of Lady Gwendolyn occurred more than once.

In the same calm voice as before, Clara asked, "Is there to be a match in that quarter? Such a long trip repeated frequently seems to suggest it. What is Lady Gwendolyn's last name?"

"Dunbar, old Lord Heather's daughter. No, it has not been quite settled I believe, but likely he will offer. His mama, I know, is anxious to see him settle down, and *not* with his local flirt."

Clara was not surprised to hear that the dashing Allingcote had a string of girls. It was exactly what she expected of him, and she asked with waning interest which lady was assumed to have the upper hand.

"He always says he will not marry Lady Gwendolyn, but then he keeps going back to Scotland, so what is to be made of it? A man does not go to a well unless he plans to drink; that is what *I* say. Gwendolyn is squat, poor thing. They so often are, the Scottish girls. I believe the cold climate stunts them, but Gwendolyn is especially compact. About four feet, eleven inches. Quite a little pygmy."

"Allingcote is tall himself. He must be six feet, I should think."

"Yes, he takes after his papa. Peg's husband was tall, but then so is Peg. The whole family are tall as trees. He and Gwen will look a horse and a dog walking together."

"How about his local flirt? What is she like?" Clara asked, selecting another card and speaking desultorily, as though just making conversation.

"Oh, she is the beauty of the region, the top heiress, and all the rest of it."

"I am surprised his mother dislikes the connection then," Clara said, surprised.

"So am I, for his papa was known to favor it, and usually old Lord Allingcote's wish is law, even if he is dead. So unnecessary," she added, looking at her bleak walls. "But Peg has taken the girl in dislike for some reason. I don't know just what it is."

Clara was interested to hear more, but disliked to enter into a pointed quizzing with her shrewd companion. She said, "Has your sister any other children?"

"Oh my yes! Three girls, all giants, and a younger son, Nickie. But Allingcote is the eldest. We call him Benjie, or Ben. He was named after Benjamin Franklin, who was a friend of his papa."

Clara had not gotten on a first-name basis with

Lord Allingcote. He had asked her to drop the "Lord," she remembered. "Lord me no lords, Miss Christopher," he had said, in his strangely imperative way. "I always feel I have escaped from the *Book of Common Prayer.*" "Do you see much of your sister's family?" Clara asked.

"We usually exchange a visit once a year. We all go to Braemore in autumn, and Peg brings the children here in the spring." Bad timing again, Clara thought. "Benjie comes, too, though he does not usually stay the whole two weeks. He was here last July by himself, but went darting off to Brighton halfway through the visit. He is strangely restless."

Clara bit back a howl of dismay. She had been in Brighton in June! Why could he not have gone in June? Her pen had proceeded to another name on the list, and this interesting subject was dropped.

It rose again a week later when Lady Allingcote, Lady Lucker's sister Peg, sent in an acceptance to the wedding invitation. She was to come with Marguerite, her eldest daughter, to arrive on the twenty-sixth of December. A few exceptions to the rule of a three-day visit were tolerated within the close family. A sister would be a useful creature to have around the house to share last-minute wedding preparations.

The two ladies were once again in the library, working on a list. On this occasion they were endeavoring to juggle a list of rooms and expected guests, the latter far exceeding the former. "I didn't realize Oglethorpe had so blasted many relatives," Lady Lucker said. Clara, being one of those relatives, said

14

nothing. "I am glad Peg is not bringing all her brood with her," Lady Lucker continued. "Children are an infernal nuisance."

"Just the two Allingcotes then, your sister and Marguerite?" Clara asked. The name Ben had not crossed her lips since its first mention a week before, but it had often been in her mind. "They could share a room, could they not?"

"I always give Peg the green suite. Maggie will take the dressing room, but I have no positive word on Ben. He was off visiting again. Peg forwarded his card somewhere or other. If he does not get it, she says he will be home for Christmas, and she will give him the message. She thinks he will come. He has had an invitation from Scotland, and is eager for an excuse to decline it."

Clara kept her head lowered, for she had a strong notion that her eyes were sparkling with pleasure.

"See what she says: 'Ben is looking for an excuse to evade the Scottish squab.' That is Lady Gwen, poor thing. And she's pigeon-chested, too. Really a regular little squab. But rich, of course. Very well to grass. So if Ben comes, that will take up the gold suite, and where do we put Oglethorpe's Uncle Maximilian?"

"Put him well away from the ladies, ma'am. Uncle Max is a pincher," Clara warned her.

"Is he indeed! And he a magistrate. If he is that sort of reprobate, I shall make him share a suite. He can share with Ben, and the two of them can help each other find out all the pretty girls. Much luck they'll have. As I glance over this list, it strikes me

15

there isn't a single beauty coming. *You* may well find yourself the belle of the ball, Clara."

"If that is a compliment, ma'am, I thank you," Clara said, laughing.

"There is nothing amiss with your looks, Clara. So Max the pincher goes in with Ben. Ben must take the dressing room and sleep on a truckle bed. He will cut up stiff over that. He is a great cutup, but very fond of Prissie. I wonder what he will give her. Peg says she will wait till they get here to buy a present after she sees what Prissie wants. I wonder if we may expect two gifts, or if they'll go snacks. Two, I shouldn't doubt. They are both awfully fond of Prissie."

The talk turned to other guests, and no definite word was received of Allingcote's coming. Clara was fully occupied during the ensuing days, overseeing the arrangement of cots and beds for the guests, getting mats ironed to cover scratched dresser tops in seldom-used rooms, and seeing to the airing of the beds.

Through all this busy time, Prissie was treated like a duchess. She sat in state in the gold saloon, serving tea to callers, shopping endlessly, and thumbing through fashion magazines and home-furnishing catalogs. She never stirred a finger to help her mama and Clara prepare her party. She sighed wearily to be put to the bother of delivering an opinion on anything. Clara had to wonder at this blind spot in Lady Lucker's makeup. She would squeeze some use out of any chance caller. Every resident within miles had some little function to fill, but

16

Prissie just sat there, the cause of all the furor, looking pained at having to say "please" or "thank you," and often neglecting even that.

The days left little time to think of Lord Allingcote, but Clara thought of him at night in her bed—a different bed now in a different room. Her former suite had been turned over to Oglethorpe's parents. She wondered if Allingcote would come. It would be placing too much significance on a brief flirtation to say that Allingcote had been in love with her. Yes, really it would be presumptuous to think anything of the sort. He had seemed to like her—had more than once sought out her company in a rather marked way at the Bellinghams'.

There, at a large house party including several attractive heiresses, the most eligible, most handsome, most absolutely desirable gentleman at the whole party had selected her as a special friend for all of three days. He had walked, talked, danced, and flirted with her. And then before the production of *The Tempest* had been staged, he had left very abruptly. His father had taken ill, she heard, and died a month later. She had not seen Allingcote since.

The memory of his well-shaped, dark head was sharply etched in her mind. She could remember it as seen from any angle. She knew to a degree at what slant his eyebrows rose up from his smoky gray eyes, knew precisely the lineaments of his nose, strong jaw, and chin. She recalled how he walked with a careless lounge and inclined his head toward anyone to whom he was speaking, because he was taller than most.

She knew too that if he came, she would be hard-pressed to keep up any show of disinterest. With not a real beauty at the party, it seemed possible he might again favor her for his flirt. She knew she was a ninny to feel such pleasure at the possibility. He had been dashing around the countryside making up to every girl he met. Traveling all the way to Scotland to see the Scottish squab, whom he had no intention of marrying. And there was his local flirt, whoever she might be. But there was no point worrying; by the twenty-fourth of December, it was still not clear whether he was coming at all. On Christmas Eve day, a card arrived saying he would stop in on the twenty-sixth, with Miss Muldoon.

That he was bringing an uninvited guest put Lady Lucker sadly out of frame. "Who the devil is Miss Muldoon?" she demanded. She sat with Prissie and Clara, trying to discover from Prissie whether she could tolerate having a new mauve mohair shawl packed in her trunk. The Highlands, where the honeymoon was to take place, would be cold, especially in winter.

"She's that girl he's been running around with for two years," Prissie said. Miss Priscilla was elegant but she was not amiable. Her smooth blond curls, her pale blue eyes, and her clear complexion were all marred by the sullen expression she wore. Her lips thinned and her nose drew down, ruining what might otherwise have been a passably pretty face. "The one Aunt Peggie hates so much, and they think

18

Ben's going to marry. You remember I told you, Mama, she was with me at Miss Simpson's Seminary."

"Ah, I knew I had heard the name before. So that's who she is. Peg usually calls her Nel; it was the Muldoon that threw me off. Old Anglin's ward—a niece, I believe. He was visiting Braemore recently. It seems it has come to a match, if Ben is bringing her here. A fine time he has chosen for it! Why could he not have married her at least, so they would only take up one room?"

Clara remembered hearing the girl spoken of as a beauty, and her hopes of being the belle of the party and enjoying a flirtation with Allingcote withered to dust. Determined to know the worst, she said to Prissie, "What does she look like?"

"Blond hair like spun silk and big blue eyes," Prissie said sullenly.

"Why, she sounds like you!" Lady Lucker exclaimed, smiling fondly at her daughter. Clara began reconsidering. If Nel Muldoon proved to be no prettier than Prissie . . .

"She is a horrid flirt," Prissie said, offended.

"Just what Benjie would like," Lady Lucker decided. "He always favored blondes, like you, Prissie. Poor Gwendolyn has that ugly brindled hair. They call her a redhead, but it is brindled like a cat. Well, Peggie may not like Nel Muldoon, but the girl is well dowered and pretty. What else can she want?"

"None of the girls at Miss Simpson's liked her," Prissie said comprehensively.

"Naturally they would not like a pretty young

heiress," her mother rallied. "Put you all in the shade, I wager. It is clear she has caught Benjie, however, and where the deuce are we to put her? Every room in the house is full to the rafters. I think she must bunk in with you, Prissie."

"No! She will not!" Prissie declared at once. "She will have her abigail and ten trunks with her. I won't have her taking over my room, right at my wedding time. I hate her."

"Oh dear," Lady Lucker said, and immediately backed down. "But we cannot send her to an inn, a single young lady, and Anglin's ward." Her mind ran to Clara's present room. Such a shabby little corner, with no space for an abigail and ten trunks, or even two. She continued to fret over this detail while Christmas approached, with all the fuss of food and Christmas baskets and carolers.

Lord Oglethorpe arrived on the evening of the twenty-fourth to spend Christmas with them, but it was the twenty-sixth that was to see the first large influx of visitors. On Christmas day they had no more than Lord Oglethorpe added to their party, and a poor addition he was, in Clara's opinion. A tall, gangly, silly fellow who fortunately spent most of his waking hours in secret conclave with Prissie in various dim corners, clutching her hand, her arm, shoulder, or waist, and whispering in her ear of the bliss awaiting them.

Clara and Lady Lucker, too, were ready to crown him, but as there were no outside visitors to see how foolishly he behaved, they tried to ignore him. Sir James, who was a collector of Roman coins, remained all unaware of the hubbub around him. He had picked up a piece of bent metal in his pasture and was busily shining it to look for traces of a head or a date, thinking he found an addition for his collection. Its size and smooth edges suggested an English crown to Clara, but she didn't tell him so.

She and Lady Lucker soon turned their attention to the more pressing matter of arranging a place in the pantry for the wedding feast that was arriving in bowls, on platters, and in boxes from all corners of the diocese. It was Clara's job to keep a list of items, along with their receptacle and owner, for the purpose of sending thanks and returning the container. She helped her hostess decide which comestibles to serve before the wedding, lest they perish into inedibility.

It was a huge, full-time task that left very little freedom to consider the unknown Miss Muldoon. A room for her had been found under the eaves, and if she did not like it, Lady Lucker said bluntly, she could lump it. She was becoming irritable from nervous exhaustion, and even said, though she didn't mean it, that she was sorry she had ever decided to "do" Prissie's wedding herself.

Clara, privy now to all the family secrets, was sent scrambling through bare linen cupboards and even ragbags to find a set of sheets for Miss Muldoon and a clean pair of towels. It was necessary to unpack the latter from Prissie's trousseau. Clara was asked to remind Lady Lucker to have them laundered and returned before the trunk left. She made a note of it and added a splinter of dislike in the fence she was building around Miss Muldoon.

When finally the twenty-sixth came, Clara was fagged with work and worry, but she was aware all the same of a coil of excitement that had nothing to do with the approaching wedding. A nervous agitation seethed within her while she went about her duties with an outward calm. Not since her childhood birthdays had she felt this mingled anticipation and apprehension, wondering if she would get the gift she craved or some well-meaning substitution. It was childish and unworthy of a grown lady, she told herself, but nothing calmed the feeling. This was the day Allingcote was to arrive, and she was on tiptoe to see him again.

Chapter Three

None of the promised guests arrived early on the twenty-sixth of December. If the guest lived nearby, he would come on the day of the wedding. The guests from afar would leave their homes in the morning and arrive late in the afternoon. Lady Allingcote and her daughter, Lady Marguerite, arrived at four o'clock. Clara was curious to see Allingcote's family. The ladies were both exceedingly stylish. The mama was not unlike Lady Lucker in appearance—tall, dark hair and eyes, full-figured, and jolly, but perhaps less talkative than her sister. Marguerite was handsome and gave some idea how the older women would have looked thirty years before, with a smooth cheek, a firm chin, and a larger, clearer eye than they could now boast.

Mother and daughter bustled in, full of good wishes and questions and a great eagerness to meet "him," Baron Oglethorpe. No sooner were their capes and bonnets off than they went to seek him out. They soon ran him to earth in the study, sitting before a blazing grate, his fingers entwined in Prissie's. Clara observed their expectant smiles dwindle to a polite parting of the lips as they ran their eyes over his rangy figure and unprepossessing countenance. By the time bows and curtsies were exchanged, the ladies had uttered their congratulations and good wishes, and Oglethorpe had civilly thanked them.

Prissie then bestirred herself to ask whether it was very cold out. Lady Marguerite said not so very and asked her if she was nervous about the approaching wedding. Prissie exchanged a secret smile with her beloved and said "a little." When this ceremony was complete, there seemed little more to say. The groom said and then repeated that he was very pleased to meet them he was sure, as though the matter had been in doubt. Having established his pleasure, his talk dried up.

Lady Lucker tried to prolong the meeting by mentioning the honeymoon in the Highlands and the fear of a cold climate. Her sister already knew the reason for this destination, but asked anyway and was told by Lady Lucker that Oglethorpe's grandma wished to meet the bride. Once it had been added that Oglethorpe's parents would be arriving the next day, ingenuity gave way to impatience and the hostess suggested a nice hot cup of tea for the travelers. It was with a sense of relief that they escaped, and the visitors were forced to exert their wits to find a compliment on the groom.

"He seems very nice" was the best they could do. Lady Allingcote, being a sister, felt free to add, "He is quiet, is he not? A little shy of strangers, I daresay."

"He will open up when he gets to know you. He has a sense of humor," Lady Lucker assured her. His reputation as a jokesmith was based on his having once put on Prissie's bonnet for a prank. It looked well on him.

Clara, temporarily free from duties, tagged along with them to the gold saloon. Lady Lucker explained in a meaningful way that Clara was Oglethorpe's cousin, which had a restraining effect on the anticipated coze. Not another word about the groom was uttered. "Has Benjie arrived yet?" Lady Allingcote asked instead.

"No, but he comes today, and do tell me, Peg," Lady Lucker asked eagerly, "is he engaged to Nel Muldoon?"

"Indeed he is not!" the mother said vehemently. "Anglin is trying to push him into it. He has Benjie there three days out of four, but it has not come to a match."

"I see. Then pray, why is he bringing her here for the wedding?"

Lady Allingcote did not swoon. Her reaction was rather an increase of spirits than a fading away. "You never mean the minx has convinced him to bring her here!" she declared noisily. Then she turned to her daughter. "Maggie, did I not say when his carriage turned off at the crossroad that he was going to say good-bye to her? It was Anglin's he was headed to certainly, and not daring to say a word to me, the wretch. To bring her here, uninvited—and at such a time! He knew I would stop him if he told me. That is why he kept silent. This is some of Nel's jiggery. Ben isn't on to half her curves. What a trick to play on you, Charity."

"We will be happy to have her," Lady Lucker said. She was not so much happy as extremely curious to see why an objection was being raised to a pretty young heiress of good birth.

"No, you will not!" Lady Marguerite laughed. "Nel will have the place in an uproar the whole time she is here."

Lady Lucker asked what was wrong with the girl, and Lady Allingcote gave her an ocular hint that it would be discussed later, when they were alone. Clara would have liked very well to hear all the details, but was discreet almost to a fault and excused herself at once.

"Why don't you run along with Clara, Maggie?" Lady Lucker suggested. "She will show you your room." She was a little ashamed at the way Oglethorpe's cousin was being used. If Clara was to dig in and work like family, she ought to be given the family privilege of gossip.

Lady Marguerite, already aware of Miss Muldoon's history, went along with Clara. She liked what she had seen of Miss Christopher thus far. "So you are Oglethorpe's cousin," she mentioned. "You don't seem much like him."

"Thank you," Clara replied, and laughed lightly. "I think that was meant for a compliment." To disassociate herself from this person who had failed to find favor with the Allingcotes, she added, "We are not at all close."

"He seems very nice," Lady Marguerite said dutifully.

"Prissie thinks so in any case." It was a relief that she was not the only one with an objectionable relation.

"She would," Lady Marguerite replied with a conspiratorial twinkle. The farce of politeness was over with and they could get down to becoming properly acquainted.

"Cousins can be so horrid," she continued, "and only because they are cousins, one is expected to like them, and be forever visiting them and writing letters. I adore Aunt Charity, the old Tartar. Prissie must take after Uncle James. In fact, all the children do. Emily, the older sister, is another oyster, and Charles, the son and heir, cannot tear himself away from Parliament for his own sister's wedding, so that gives you some idea."

"He has been set the task of drawing up some bill or other, Sir James says. I have been here six weeks and have not seen him yet."

"Count your blessings."

Clara showed Lady Marguerite to her room. The maid was busy unpacking her trunk, so they went along to Clara's room to talk. "Good gracious! Are you sleeping in this little cubbyhole?" Lady Marguerite exclaimed.

"Just for the time being, while the wedding guests are here."

"It is really too bad of Benjie to bring Nel, landing

in here at such a time, but I suppose he didn't know how crowded it would be."

Clara, keenly interested in this line of talk, said, "It will be an excellent time for him to introduce Miss Muldoon to the family, will it not? If he is to marry her, he will want all the family to get to know her."

"I suppose so."

"Your mama does not favor the notion at all, I gather?"

"No. Mama already knows her."

"What—what exactly is amiss with her?" Clara asked quietly.

Lady Marguerite rolled her eyes and said, "You'll see."

Clara was inclined to seek further details, but as her new friend immediately ran into a new and equally interesting line of gossip, she did not try to divert her. Lady Marguerite told, without a bit of prodding, how much nicer all Benjie's other flirts were. A whole raft of Miss this and Lady that and Cousin so-and-so flew from her tongue, till Clara's head was spinning. What a fool she had been to think Allingcote meant a thing by his attentions to her. He was a gazetted flirt, who spent his days flitting about from house to house, visiting any family with a nubile daughter.

They talked for thirty minutes, at the end of which time Lady Marguerite went to her room to clean up after her trip, and Clara went belowstairs to see if she was needed and to see as well, of course, if Miss Muldoon and her escort had arrived yet.

Clara had been gone scarcely half an hour, but during that short interval many carriages had arrived and unloaded the occupants, who swarmed about the entranceway, the gold saloon, and even up the stairs. Many of the visitors were strangers to Clara, but Oglethorpe's relations were hers also, and she knew them. She had spent time in many of their homes and had to seek these relatives out for a friendly word explaining what she was doing here at Branelea. She was introduced to the Lucker relations—the names familiar to her from writing invitations, as well as various lists.

Accustomed to meeting many strangers as she was, Clara enjoyed this free-for-all. Her mind was quick to fit a name to a face, and with a leg in both the Lucker and Oglethorpe camps, she was soon busy making introductions of her own. So busy that she failed to remark the gentleman in the far corner of the room, observing her every move and trying to catch her eye.

She didn't even know Lord Allingcote was there, while his gray eyes first widened in disbelief, then crinkled at the edges in a smile, and finally narrowed in impatience. Till he rose and lounged toward her at a familiar gait, with his well-shaped head preceding his shoulders a little, she didn't even see him. But as soon as Lord Allingcote was seen, he was recognized, and she stopped dead in the middle of welcoming her Cousin Esmeralda to stare at him, as if he were a ghost.

In two paces he was at her side, bowing and saying in his familiar offhand way, "Fancy meeting you here, Miss Christopher!" The warmth of his voice removed any casual air from the trite remark. That, and his remembering her name after two years.

"Oh, Lord Allingcote, you remember me," she said, and dropped a curtsy.

"Remember you!" he exclaimed, shocked. "But of course! Well, well, small world, isn't it?" he said, then emitted a laugh that was a little too loud and sounded almost nervous—so unlike his usual social polish. "Have I left out any of the customary banalities?" he asked her with a smile. "We've had 'fancy meeting you here' and 'small world.' I had no idea you would be here. I didn't realize you were a friend of Prissie's."

"I'm not. That is—I am now I hope—but I am here because of Oglethorpe. He is my cousin."

"Is he indeed? No one told me that. What a pleasant surprise this is, seeing you again." He put his hand on her elbow and continued, "Won't you join me in that quiet little corner there between the palms, that I have usurped for myself? Quite a tropical oasis in the desert of Auntie's saloon, with a good bottle of claret standing by. You don't remember, I suppose, my predilection for claret at the Bellinghams', but I remember *you* always preferred sherry, and shall procure you a glass if you'll join me among the palms."

His friendly interest, his remembering where they had met before, and even her preference for sherry, amazed her. Clara was so overcome she could hardly reply. While she hesitated, he went on, "Do come. We have so much to talk about, and at a big do like this, you need not worry about mixing with everyone. I have been hiding for thirty minutes and no one has missed me." As he spoke, he led her to the palm trees in the corner, magically picking a glass of sherry off a passing tray along the way. Soon they were seated, a little apart from the others, looking at each other with conscious, almost shy glances.

Clara racked her brain for something to say, but the only thing she could think of was Nel Muldoon, and she disliked to let him know she had been gossiping about him.

"How did *The Tempest* go on after I left?" he asked. "I was called away suddenly. I hadn't even time to say good-bye to you—to anyone except Lady Bellingham, in fact."

"We heard about your father, and were sorry to hear it. The play went on fine. Someone—Boo Withers I think it was—took your part. Well, you hadn't a very large part, as I recall."

"They knew what they were about to cast me as one of the attendant lords. I am no actor. And you were to be one of the spirits. Iris, was it not? You should have been Miranda, the leading lady."

He even remembered the insignificant little part she had been cast to play. "Oh no! That was the only important female role in the play. Miss Bellingham played it marvelously."

"Just like Buck Bellingham to put on a play with no good roles for ladies, when he had the very flower of Albion's womanhood assembled under his roof at the time. He had that charming Kessler girl play Sycorax, with her blond curls all stuffed up under a fright wig. He should have put on *The Taming of the Shrew* or *The Merry Wives of Windsor*."

Clara saw that his memory was as keen for other girls at the party as herself, and her joy was diluted accordingly. "What Buck really wanted was to get himself rigged out as Caliban and scare the wits out of everyone," she replied. "He did it very well, too."

"What have you been doing since then, Miss Christopher? That was two years ago, and I haven't had a glimpse of you since. I heard you had gone to Scotland for a visit."

"I was there for a few months. Then I was at Devon for six weeks."

His shaking head indicated mild disapproval, but his smile was warm. "Still on the move, I see. I know you dislike gathering moss, but this constant shifting about must also make it difficult to gather friends. Where are you staying now, tumbleweed?"

She laughed in surprise at his having hit on her secret name for herself. "How did you know I call myself the human tumbleweed?"

"You told me. Don't you remember? That afternoon you were making Caliban's headpiece from an old mop, using me as your plaster blockhead. You told me I had the best blockhead at the party. I was highly flattered."

"You're making that up. I never said anything of the sort I'm sure." She found herself laughing again at his lively nonsense. She didn't remember the occasion in detail, but had some recollection of making Caliban's headpiece, and how else could he know she

32

called herself the tumbleweed, if she hadn't told him?

"Indeed you did! A man doesn't get a compliment like that every day—thank God. I remember it very well. And I bet I remember something else you've forgotten."

"What is that?" The absurd idea danced into her head that he was going to remember her rose gown and pay some exaggerated compliment on it.

"You promised—" He paused, and changed his mind. "No, think a moment. See if you can remember what you were supposed to do." He looked closely at her, his gray eyes quizzical, while a soft smile played over his lips.

Her mind ran back to that visit two years ago. She remembered being in conversation with Allingcote several times. She recalled how he looked, the tone of his voice, she remembered laughing a great deal, but the meetings were not much differentiated from one another. She remembered she had a wonderful time, but no specific words, certainly nothing in the nature of a promise. She shook her head.

"You have a shockingly bad memory, Miss Christopher. You promised you would write me out the words of "The Maid of Lodi," that we might entertain the company with a duet. And you didn't do it. I daresay you took a bribe from someone. There was a petition going around to block us, if I remember aright."

"Well sir, if my memory is shockingly bad, I must own yours is shockingly good. It must be almost an inconvenience to have so much useless lumber stored up in your head."

"The old blockhead is selective. It only remembers the good things—like broken promises." There was a tinge of accusation in his voice.

"You can hardly hold me responsible for that. You left," Clara pointed out.

"True, I must acquit you of accepting bribery. But did you ever write out the words? I wager you did not. You know, I think, where they might have been forwarded? I have outwitted the world, however, and learned the words by myself. I sing it wherever I go. People plug their ears when they see me approach, music in hand, and dash for the closest exit. I plan to stun the assembly this evening with a rendition. Perhaps you will join me?"

"I must confess, this old head of mine has forgotten the words, if it ever knew them."

"I'll write them out for you—and *I* won't break my promise either," he said, gazing deeply into her eyes. After a moment, Allingcote shook himself to attention. "But we have detoured from what I was asking you. Where are you staying now?"

"Here."

"I mean after the wedding. Where are you *living* nowadays?"

"I am living here for two months," she said, and went on to explain about her aunt's wedding trip.

He looked stunned. "You mean you have been with Aunt Charity for six weeks!"

"Yes, and shall be for two more."

"But why didn't she—why didn't *you* let me know?

Braemore is only fifty miles away. We might have met any number of times."

"I believe your mama was aware that I have been staying here," she replied, in a little confusion. "We have been very busy with Prissie's wedding, and have not done much entertaining."

"Mama didn't tell me you were here. Of course she didn't know I—you—that we are acquainted," he said, flustered. "I daresay that explains it. And you will be here for two more weeks, you say?"

"Yes, till mid-January. That is, we are going to London for New Year's to visit Sir James's Uncle Percy, but will be returning shortly afterward."

"And after that?" he asked with a strange eagerness. "I mean to get your itinerary quite straight this time, so you don't tumble away on me again," he said, with flattering eagerness. "Do you return to Sussex, to the aunt who is presently in Greece?"

"Yes, as soon as she is settled. They have not chosen a house yet. Both had hired apartments that they have let go."

"This is no good. You don't actually know *where* you'll be. You'll take off to Scotland or somewhere . . . But I'll be here till the thirtieth. We'll be meeting any number of times. In any case, you can always be in touch with me at Braemore. If, by any chance, you are spirited off by your aunt, *do* let me know where you are staying. A simple note directed to me at home will settle everything. We shall not consider it a clandestine correspondence. Here, I'll give you the direction." He pulled a card from his pocket and saw it put in her own before proceeding to any other matter.

They chatted on in the most amiable way for a quarter of an hour. The two-year interval since the visit at the Bellinghams' might never have been. They were back on the same easy footing, with Allingcote paying her the same marked attentions as formerly. In Clara's mind the word "love" did not seem so presumptuous as it had seemed before his coming. She admitted, however, that flirtation might be a better word, considering his clear memory of other flirts as well.

Still, certain details that emerged lent a stronger inference than mere dalliance to his conduct. His insistence that she be able to get in touch with him by some means, his apparently genuine chagrin at not knowing she had been so close for six weeks, and even more than these, his sharp recollection of all the details of their relationship at the Bellinghams'. Surely a flirt would require a prodigious memory to store up such details of *all* his flirts.

"I really must go," Clara said reluctantly. She had twice caught Lady Lucker's eye on her. There were certain arrangements regarding rooms and dinner that Clara was to check out.

"So soon? You just got here! You've hardly looked around the island at all," he urged, pointing to the two palm trees in pots. "I thought we might explore a little, when the sun goes down. There might be buried gold . . ."

"I have some things I must be doing," she insisted, and rose.

Allingcote got up and put a detaining hand on her elbow. "Let me help you. I'll be bored to flinders here with all these relatives and strangers. I hardly know which is worse. It really isn't fair of you to run off and leave me abandoned alone on a desert island. No ship to rescue me."

"I never heard of an oasis on a desert island."

"You may never see another. Stay awhile. I'll climb the trees and pick you coconuts—mangoes. They're really marvelous trees."

She removed his hand and began walking away. Allingcote tagged along. A matter that had been occupying some large part of Clara's mind finally came out in speech. "What about Miss Muldoon? You should not abandon her to what must be a whole roomful of strangers."

The effect of her speech was dramatic. Allingcote came to a dead halt. His eyes took on a frightened or guilty look. His hand went to his forehead and he exclaimed, "Good God, I forgot all about Nellie."

Clara's soaring hopes began to plunge.

Chapter Four

Guilt was definitely the expression Allingcote wore as he looked around the room for his precious Nellie. And well he might feel guilty, flirting his head off with her for the better part of half an hour. He scanned the floor carefully, then turned back to Clara with his old dégagé smile. "It's all right. She went upstairs to see Prissie, but I feared she might have come back down. They are old school chums, fortunately. Otherwise, I could not have brought her here at such a time."

Clara was curious to hear why he had brought her, uninvited, but could not like to inquire directly. "I suppose I had best go after her," he said, following Clara across the room. At the doorway they met Lady Lucker wearing a distracted face.

"Ben, Clara, I must speak to you. The ghastliest thing has happened!"

"Oh Lord, it's not Nel?" Ben asked. An expression of panic seized his face. It spoke clearly of a great concern for the girl.

Lady Lucker rushed them into the privacy of the

hall to unfold the tale. "No, it is not Nel. What must happen but those two geese, Georgiana and Gertrude Snelley, have made the trip from London, expecting to be put up here after as well as saying they would not come. They got a free ride, that is what did the mischief. Not a square inch of space in the house. There simply isn't a nook or cranny I can squeeze them into, unless I put them in the cellar with the hogsheads and black beetles."

"Give them my room," Ben said at once. "I meant to tell you when I brought Miss Muldoon, Auntie, that I would put up at an inn. The One-Eyed Jack is not above a mile away. I shall stay there and take along someone else with me, if you need two rooms."

"A good idea," Lady Lucker said at once. "You are sharing the gold suite with Oglethorpe's Uncle Maximilian—a truckle bed in the dressing room, I fear." She stopped and shook her head. "I am so rattled, my wits are gone begging. I cannot put Georgiana and Gertrude in a room adjoining Maximilian's. He pinches."

"They'll love it," Ben grinned. "No, don't hit the roof, Auntie. I was only joking. You can shift the guests about somehow," he went on, with typical masculine obtuseness on domestic matters.

"We have shifted and sorted till we are blue in the face," his aunt snapped. "There is no way. Prissie refuses to share with your friend, Miss Muldoon, because of hating her so, and I must say . . ."

Ben leapt on it like a hound on a bone. "*Hating her!* Nellie said they were great friends. Quite the bosomest of bows. I wondered Prissie hadn't asked her to the wedding. Nel thought it must be an over-sight."

His aunt stared at him as if he were a bedlamite. "Oh no, everyone at Miss Simpson's Seminary hated Miss Mul—Oh dear! Now don't take a pet, Benjie. She is monstrously pretty, your Miss Muldoon. It was jealousy like as not, that set all the girls against her. Of course we are happy to have her."

"The little minx," Allingcote said, with a smile that showed not a single trace of disapproval. It almost verged on admiration. "She told me that whisker on purpose to get me to bring her. I am frightfully sorry, Auntie. What can I do to help?"

"I don't know," she replied glumly. Before more could be said, there was a racket in the doorway of the study. Three people came out, one well in advance of the others. Prissie led the way, her blue eyes flashing. Behind her straggled Oglethorpe and a blond Incomparable, hanging possessively on his arm and looking as smug as a cat with a new litter.

"I must speak to you, Mama—*alone*," Prissie said, and jostling past the others, she pulled her mama into the study and slammed the door after them. She promptly burst into tears and declared that if Miss Muldoon did not leave the house that instant, she would—the consequences were lost in sniffles, but it was obviously some such dire fate as suicide or breaking off the marriage or perhaps murder that she had in mind. Lady Lucker comforted her as best she could and rashly promised to be rid of the girl.

The scene on the other side of the door was less melodramatic, but hardly more pleasant for Clara.

40

Allingcote and Oglethorpe were slightly acquainted; Miss Christopher and Miss Muldoon had to be introduced to each other. The meeting was accomplished with the liveliest curiosity on Clara's part, and very little on Miss Muldoon's. The girl, Clara soon saw, was the eighth wonder of the world.

She put every female Clara had ever met in the shade, and she had met a great many pretty ladies in her travels. The most surprising thing about Nel was her delicacy. She looked like a finely wrought porcelain statue. Her skin had that white, translucent quality of fine china, with a light pink tinge on the cheeks. A tousle of blond curls fell free about her face in a wanton way. Her little pink lips opened to reveal faultless teeth, and her diminutive body was gowned in a pale blue lutestring creation inspired, Clara thought, by Watteau, and executed by some latter-day French wizard.

The word "apparition" came to mind upon first seeing her. She seemed more a celestial vision than crude, mortal flesh and blood. When Clara had gazed her fill, she glanced at the two gentlemen and noticed that they too were struck into muteness by her beauty. Oglethorpe was regarding her with his mouth hanging slack, a highly unappetizing sight, quite apart from his position as Prissie's groom. Allingcote looked bewitched as he inquired in tones of mock severity, "What have you been up to now, Nel, to get Prissie in an uproar?" The speech suggested her standard way of behaving was to cause an uproar wherever she went.

"I can't imagine why Prissie is upset," Miss Muldoon said innocently. "We were all having such a nice coze, were we not, Oglethorpe? I was just recalling how Prissie had such ugly spots in school, though she has nearly recovered." She spoke in the soft, breathless voice of a child, but there was mature feminine guile in her flashing eyes that smiled a secret message at Oglethorpe.

Oglethorpe turned beet red. "Miss Muldoon tells me you are taking her to London, Allingcote."

"Yes, we are on our way there," he replied.

That was his only excuse for having imported this piece of mischief into the household. At least he had enough sense not to repeat the faradiddle that Nel and Prissie were bosom bows. London was only a few hours away, whereas the wedding was still three days off. Why did he not take her to London and return alone? It was the only sane course, and if Clara had been the hostess instead of a guest, she would have suggested it.

It was perfectly obvious that Nel Muldoon was a mischief maker of no mean proportions. She scarcely glanced at Clara. The smallest of curtsies was her only acknowledgment. Her attention was all for the gentlemen, three-quarters of it for Oglethorpe, though Allingcote received an occasional bat of the fan or ridiculously long eyelashes. She called him Benjie, in a drawling way. Clara was stymied to determine the relationship between them. They were on a very familiar pet-name basis, with an air of flirtation on the lady's side at least. Allingcote's attitude was more difficult to gauge. He clearly admired Nel, but his admiration had something of the avuncular about it. It was a sort of smiling tolerance that Clara thought might be an attitude developed to mask chronic jealousy.

When Nel latched onto Oglethorpe's arm and tried to walk off with him, the tolerance was at an end. "That'll be enough of that, Nel," he said sharply, and taking her arm, he tucked it firmly under his own, patting her hand. Nel smiled up at him through her lashes. Clara felt a strong urge to strike her.

"I had best speak to Lady Lucker," Clara said, and walked briskly toward the study door. Oglethorpe followed her, but was barred at the entrance by Prissie's mama, who did not wish him to get a view of Prissie's red eyes and angry face. Till the vows were exchanged, she could not relax her vigilance a moment.

"We shall be out directly," Lady Lucker said. "Go and see if your mama is quite comfortable, Oglethorpe."

He was not tardy to nip off and try to catch up to Miss Muldoon, who had walked off with Allingcote.

Lady Lucker pulled Clara into the room and closed the door. "Clara, what is to be done?" was her distracted salutation. "Prissie positively refuses to have Miss Muldoon under the roof, telling Oglethorpe about her spots. And how can I put the minx out? Ben's special friend, fiancée very likely. And now Georgiana and Gertrude landing in on us unannounced, after sending a flannalette nightgown. It is really too much. I thank God I have no more daughters to be bounced off. This wedding will be the death of me."

"We shall contrive somehow, ma'am, never fear," Clara said with a calmness that took a deal of effort. It was the "fiancée very likely" that caused it.

"Really it is unthinking of Ben to bring her at such a time, and unlike him. The least he could do is keep her from flirting her head off with Oglethorpe."

Prissie raised her head from her moist handkerchief long enough to wail, "She called him Oggie!"

"Hussy!" Lady Lucker fumed. In her heart Clara agreed, and disliked the girl as much as either of them.

"Let us put it to Allingcote," Clara suggested. "He says he is taking her to London. He can take her and be back in time for the wedding."

"She let on she was glad to see me," Prissie said, surfacing once again from the depths of her pique. "She never liked me one bit. She only came to try to steal Oggie from me."

"And such a pretty little wretch," the mother commiserated unwisely. "But I think you have an excellent idea, Clara. I shall go and speak to Benjie at once." In her eagerness to be rid of Miss Muldoon, it did not occur to her that a single young lady and gentleman could not well set out for London with dark approaching.

It proved unnecessary to seek Allingcote out. A light tap at the door was the preface to his entry, wearing a worried frown. "What a kettle of fish I've landed in on you, Auntie. I couldn't be sorrier."

"Where is Miss Muldoon? Where's Oglethorpe?" Prissie asked sharply.

"Not together, love," Ben soothed her. "I set

Mama to guarding Nel, and Oglethorpe is with his own mama. But they'll want sharp watching, the pair of them."

Prissie broke out into a fresh concert of sobs, punctuated with indistinguishable mumbles of "kill," "hate," and "love." The three looked at her with mingled impatience and sympathy, and uttered a weary joint sigh.

"The thing is, Ben," Lady Lucker said, "we feel that as you are taking Miss Muldoon to London, the best thing is for you to get on with it and get rid of her. I mean for the time being. You can bring her back later." A jerk of her head in Prissie's direction told him clearly the reason for this uncivil suggestion.

"That would be best, of course," he agreed, "but there is at the moment no one in London to receive her. The relatives I am taking her to are out of town for Christmas, and won't be back till the thirtieth."

A wail rose louder from Prissie's handkerchief. Lady Lucker sat down and sunk her face in her hands. "It's hopeless. She will have gotten away with Oglethorpe by then. Well, if she must stay, you'll have to keep her fully occupied, Ben."

"She is not in the least interested in Oglethorpe," he said hotly. "It is only mischievousness on her part. She'll stop when I tell her it bothers Prissie."

How an otherwise sane gentleman could hold such a foolish opinion was a matter of deep mystery to the three ladies.

"She's not staying here," Prissie announced. "If she stays, I go."

"My dear," Lady Lucker clucked, and cast a desperate, pleading glance at her nephew.

"Is there any neighbor who might take her?" Clara suggested.

Lady Lucker considered this possibility, mentioning that neighbors were already putting up other guests.

"Actually," Ben said uncertainly, "I would not like Nel to be packed off just anywhere. I mean a house with young gentlemen in it—well, she is so very attractive, you know."

"We noticed, Ben," Lady Lucker said in an acid voice.

"You see I am in—in rather special care of her," Ben continued. "She is Anglin's ward. He was a good friend of Papa's, and—and I have offered—" Clara's heart squeezed painfully. "Offered to look after her till her cousins, the Bertrams, return to London."

Her heart resumed beating. His excuse was accepted and interpreted to mean it had not yet come to a definite proposal. Clara's bland face denoted not a trace of being surprised or disappointed, or even disapproving that he should have been flirting with her quite outrageously half an hour ago. If Allingcote felt his position uncomfortable, he also concealed it.

He went to Prissie and put his arm over her heaving shoulders in an effort to conciliate her and get her to accept her sworn enemy at her wedding. "She'll behave, Prissie. I'll take care to keep her out of your and Oglethorpe's way. She doesn't mean any harm. It is only her friendly way." Prissie twitched away from his arm and turned her back on the whole group. This was taken to mean her ultimatum stood.

"It does seem hard that poor Prissie must be upset at this time," her mother said, hoping still to get the hoyden out of the house.

"Indeed it does," Clara said. She had been thinking furiously, and had come up with an idea. "Is there any reason why Miss Muldoon could not stay at the inn, with myself as chaperon?" she asked. "That would leave my room and Miss Muldoon's free for Miss Georgiana and Gertrude, Lady Lucker."

"No, really!" Allingcote objected.

He was overborne by Lady Lucker's heartfelt, "The very thing! There, you hear that, Pris? Clara is taking her off to the inn."

"No, it won't do," Allingcote said firmly. "She is the very devil of a handful, Miss Christopher. There is no reason why *you* should be put out of your room, put to such great inconvenience because of my stupidity in bringing Nel here. Mama will take her."

"I don't mind in the least," Clara said, for she saw the idea appealed strongly to her hostess.

"I'll pay for the rooms," Lady Lucker volunteered, which told as clearly as words could tell how much she favored the scheme.

"No, I'll foot the bill. Nellie is my friend," Allingcote said promptly.

"I hope one of you will pay for Miss Muldoon at least," Clara said frankly, "for I have exactly one guinea and seven shillings to my name till next quarter day."

"Let Miss Muldoon pay for herself" was Prissie's

spiteful comment, but she looked definitely improved in spirits at the notion of getting the girl boarded out.

"My dear, run along and dry your eyes," Lady Lucker said. "And see if you can find Oglethorpe." Prissie left, and the other three remained behind to hammer out the details of the remove to the inn.

Chapter Five

"You cannot stay locked up with Nellie in an inn all day long, Miss Christopher," Allingcote began. "She is so full of life she wants to be out and doing. And in any case, she will want to be with me, as we are—that is, as I am the only friend she has in town."

As a perpetually floating houseguest, Clara had encountered many unintended slurs, but never one that stung so sharply as Allingcote's. For a fleeting moment she had thought it was *her* ennui he was worried about. But no, *she* could stay locked up in an inn forever; it was Miss Muldoon, bursting with life, who must have livelier entertainment. And that entertainment must be provided by her escort, Allingcote. Clara was glad her hostess replied, for she could not trust herself to be civil much longer.

"Nonsense!" the dame declared. "Clara cannot stay away all day long. I need her for a million jobs. There is the seating arrangement for the wedding dinner to be finished, Clara. You were to do that for me, and helping in the kitchen to keep track of the food coming in. You must return as soon as you are up in the morning—not too late mind. And you, Benjie, must keep your friend out of our way. Take her for drives or walks, or into the village."

Ben's spine stiffened perceptibly. "I would prefer to keep her out of the village."

"Why?" his aunt asked.

"Anglin would not like her to be traipsing about the shops."

It was too paltry an excuse for serious rebuttal, but Lady Lucker repeated that in any case she must be kept away from Branelea.

"What time shall we go to the inn?" Clara asked.

"We can hardly turn Miss Muldoon away before dinner," the hostess said regretfully.

"I'll take you both over after dinner," Allingcote told her. "I shall put up there myself, too, leaving the gold suite for Maximilian."

"That is not in the least necessary, Ben," his aunt said. "If Anglin does not want her to be seen in the shops, he sounds a proper Tartar. He would disapprove of her staying at the inn with her beau, with only Clara for chaperon."

"I am not her beau," he said, with an apologetic glance at Clara. "Why she's only a child."

"She is Prissie's age. Prissie is getting married in three days," Lady Lucker pointed out.

"Nel is only seventeen. She was behind Prissie in school."

"Be that as it may," the lady said with a disbelieving eye, "Miss Muldoon is no child."

"There is no reason for you to stay at the inn," Clara said. She had observed his apologetic glance and his quick assurance that he was not Nellie's beau and was tingling with curiosity to hear more. "I shall pack a bag and clear my things out of my room. Oh, Lady Lucker—what about linen, if the room is to be used for other guests?"

"We have time to see to all that before you go. I discovered a batch of old sheets the servants had put aside for rags and have set a maid to mending them. They'll do well enough for Gertrude, simple old ninny."

Allingcote turned to Clara. "I shall take you and Nel to the inn after dinner. I'm very sorry I have caused you so much bother. And you, too, Auntie," he added to Lady Lucker.

His aunt accepted the apology with a resigned sigh and hustled off to see to the mended linen. "You will all be wishing me at Jericho," Allingcote said to Clara, with a self-disparaging smile that invited contradiction.

She murmured some polite denial. It was only Miss Muldoon they were all wishing at Jericho. Allingcote was wishing her at the same location at that moment. "You don't know what you're letting yourself in for," he warned her. "I strongly recommend taking breakfast in your room in the morning, and I shall be there early waiting for you both belowstairs. I don't mean to imply you must rise early, only that I shall be there early, waiting."

Clara gave him a quizzing smile. "How pleasant for you."

"I am used to waiting for Nel" was his very unsatisfactory reply.

"You haven't got her very well trained, have you?"

"Her spirit is unbroken and unbent. A proper wild little filly. It is unpardonable for me to foist her off on to you. I still think I should stay at the inn. There is no impropriety in it, do you think?" His brows rose and his gray eyes, as clear as crystals, studied her.

Clara shrugged unhelpfully. "I am only an amateur chaperon—I haven't even put on my caps. Your aunt thinks it undesirable; I rather think Anglin might feel the same."

"I see your point. Who chaperons the chaperons?" he asked, rubbing his hands and leering facetiously. "But as to Anglin's taking a pet over it, he is so relieved to have her off his hands he wouldn't care if I locked her in a dungeon. In fact, he threatened to do it himself."

"What did she do?" Clara asked, her curiosity reaching a new pitch at his thoughtless comment.

For a moment, she thought he was about to tell her. He looked on the edge of some interesting revelation, then as she watched, his face became passive. "Nothing so very bad, really," he said vaguely. "She is merely high-spirited. And of course so damnably attractive she has all the beaux in a twitter, including Oglethorpe. Did you ever see such a mackerel? He on the verge of his own wedding—" He came to a conscious stop as he remembered her relationship to the groom. "I mean . . ."

She let him stammer a moment, then said, "I know what you mean. Frankly our opinion of Cousin Oglethorpe does not run high. You must not desist from denigrating him only because he is my cousin. Between your aunt and myself, we agree the only wise move he ever made was to offer for Prissie."

"Hardly an inspired piece of genius either. We all have our less-than-perfect cousins. She is hardly taking this contretemps like a lady."

"I beg to differ. She is taking it exactly as most ladies would take it."

"Not as *you* would take it, Miss Christopher, I think," he said, and smiled warmly.

"Not so very differently." She was every bit as jealous as Prissie, and she had no groom for Nel to flirt with. No, her pique was aroused that Nel chose to flirt with her own beau, and possibly husband-to-be. But what galled her even more was his lack of disapproval of Nel's behavior. Everyone was held to blame except the troublemaker.

"You appear to have got on remarkably cosy terms with Aunt Charity in a short space of time. No hiding the skeleton sheets in the closet. Do you like her?"

"I like her enormously. We are kindred spirits."

"Sister cheeseparings, eh?" he joked. "I never took you for a skint, Miss Christopher."

"The more accomplished skints conceal their vice. I taught your aunt a few tricks, and vice versa," she said playfully.

"I would like to hear more of this."

"I shall just drop you a hint, Lord Allingcote. You waste a few pennies by having your cards printed. You might cut them from a large sheet of cardboard and write them up by hand, as we did the place cards for the table. Mind you, we bought a dozen real cards for the titles who will be attending."

He studied her with a bemused smile. "I thought I knew you quite well. Not long, but well. I hope Auntie hasn't taught you to cut the wine with water. That is one of her little economies I cannot countenance. I don't mind the mended sheets and short candles, or even the two logs she leaves for the grate. Three is the minimum that will actually kindle, you know. But cut wine is an abomination."

"I shall personally see you have a bottle of undiluted claret in your chamber, sir, if it means a trip to the bowels of the cellar, which it will."

"Been elevated to butler, have you? Auntie mentioned having a million or so jobs for you. You can save yourself that one job, however. I always bring my own wine to Branelea, and have also instructed my valet to see I get at least lukewarm water in the morning."

"I hope Miss Muldoon and myself fare as well at the inn."

"You will. I'll go with you and speak to the proprietor. And Cla—Miss Christopher, let us not have any embarrassing arguments about paying the bill. You are doing me a favor by helping me look after Nel."

"Very well," she agreed, not embarrassed, but not wishing to linger on the subject either.

"There is just one little thing. I hope you don't mind adjoining rooms? I think you ought to leave the door open between, in case . . ." He didn't finish the statement, and Clara looked a sharp question at him.

"Is she subject to nightmares, or—"

54

"Yes!" he said, but too swiftly, with too much the air of grasping at a straw.

Clara studied him closely. The signs of apprehension were easy to see: the flush around the neck, the unsteady eyes. "And now perhaps you will favor me with the truth, sir?"

Allingcote seemed almost relieved to have the charade done with. "You know me too well, Miss Christopher. The fact is, she might take into her head to—well, *leave.*"

"Good gracious, a runaway! What have I gotten myself into?"

"A pack of trouble, milady!" he laughed. "No really, I don't think she'll bolt on us. Not tonight at least."

"But why would she do it at all? What sort of girl is she, Allingcote?"

"Oh she's a darling, but she requires the greatest vigilance. Are you a light sleeper, I hope?"

"I sleep like a log. Oh but I shan't close an eye tonight, I know it."

"I wish she might stay here, at Branelea. If only Prissie hadn't set her face against the plan. And that demmed jackanapes of an Oglethorpe drooling all over Nel . . ."

Clara overlooked these rationalizations. Her mind was busy trying to determine just how closely she must guard Nel. "Surely she won't try to run away with no carriage, nor anyone to help her?"

"Probably not. I'll check the hours of the stages to be sure."

"Lord Allingcote, I think you owe it to me to tell

me the whole. If I am to be responsible for the girl, I must know."

"You are *not* responsible for her. *I* am, and I *will* stay at the inn. It is too much to saddle you with."

"Well—but you cannot stay with her, with the adjoining door open as you suggested . . ."

"No, but I hope you will, and between the two of us, we'll ride herd on her so hard she won't have a chance to sheer off on us."

"This was all I needed," Clara said, and turned to walk slowly from the room.

She went upstairs to pack her bag. The many various impressions gleaned that afternoon swirled through her brain as she worked. Allingcote seemed not only happy but delighted to have met her again. His conversation suggested that he had thought of her often during the months they had been apart. Yet he was certainly mixed up in some close manner with the irresistible, the "darling" Nel Muldoon.

There was a possibility that the three of them staying at the inn was an indiscreet thing to do, but she was committed to it, and if Miss Muldoon was likely to take off into the night, she was not eager to be in sole charge of the girl. She remembered Lady Marguerite's words when she had asked what Nel was like. "You'll see," she had warned. She had already seen she was a beautiful flirt and feared what else was to be revealed in the near future.

Chapter Six

Dinner at Branelea on the twenty-sixth of December was the opening salvo of the nuptial festivities. Twenty-four persons were seated in the dining hall. To a not overly discerning eye, the table was a picture of elegance. Candlelight flickered benignly on crystal and silver and linen. Only Clara and Lady Lucker knew that the best linen tablecloth was being saved for the wedding feast. For this occasion the cloth was mended at one end where it had got caught in the paddles of the washing dolly. Miss Georgiana and Miss Gertrude could consider themselves fortunate to be at the table at all. A mended cloth was plenty good enough for these suppliers of flannalette nighties and bed jackets. Lady Lucker's supply of good china and crystal and sterling silver was sufficient to serve twenty-four, however, and her neighbors had supplied a splendid array of viands.

With Clara's help in arranging the table, Miss Muldoon was set well away from Oglethorpe. From some perverse sense of martyrdom, Clara placed Allingcote well away from herself as well. She could only observe him across the board at the far end of the table, entertaining Miss Muldoon to the top of his bent. Her small consolation was that he frequently glanced down the length of the starched linen to herself.

The meal went off without a hitch. When the ladies left the gentlemen to their port, Miss Muldoon marched straightway to Prissie. Clara was after her in a flash, to lure her off to a corner out of mischief. Lady Lucker nodded in commendation of this wise precaution and sent Lady Marguerite along to join them. Clara was happy for the ally, particularly as the two young ladies were well acquainted.

"We didn't expect to see you here, Nel," Lady Marguerite said.

Miss Muldoon gave a triumphant little smile and replied, "Benjie arranged it all with Uncle Anglin. He didn't want to be away from me for so long." By some oversight of nature, Nel lacked dimples, but she had all the other paraphernalia of the flirt. The head cocked at a coy angle, the glance up through the long lashes, the teasing smile. Even in conversation with ladies exclusively, she practiced all her winsome tricks.

"When was it arranged?" Lady Marguerite asked unconcernedly.

"When Ben was with us for the whole week before Christmas." Nel preened her hair with a fragile white hand.

"Ben was at the Dornes' last week," Lady Marguerite countered.

"For part of the week we were at the Dornes'," Nel

replied. "I convinced Benjie to take me, for I was bored to flinders waiting for Christmas to come. But he fell into one of his jealous fits when Mickey Dorne tried to set up a flirtation with me, and we left earlier than we had intended."

Her questioner shrugged and looked away, but Clara was listening avidly. It was becoming as clear as the three sides of a triangle that Nel was either engaged to Ben or about to receive an offer. Nothing else could account for his living in her pocket. Miss Muldoon turned a sharp blue eye on Miss Christopher and said, "You have known Benjie for quite a long time, have you?"

"I scarcely know him at all. We met once at a house party a few years ago."

"I thought from your manner toward him it must be rather more than that," the girl said pointedly, but still smiling. "I noticed a certain—familiarity, but then you older women are not so restricted as we young girls are."

"I haven't noticed you placing any restrictions on yourself, Nel," Lady Marguerite said, not even trying to hide her dislike. Turning to Clara she added, "You didn't mention knowing Ben, Miss Christopher. How long have you been acquainted?"

"We met two years ago. About two years ago—it was before Christmas actually."

A curious expression seized Lady Marguerite's face. "It wasn't at the Bellinghams' house party? The one where Ben had to come home unexpectedly because of Papa's illness?"

"Yes, that was the one. I haven't seen him since."

"I see," Lady Marguerite replied enigmatically. She began to examine Clara with a new, keener interest.

"It is strange Benjie should choose such a slight acquaintance to chaperon me," Nel said with an air of pique. Her manner suggested he was usually more fastidious regarding who he let near her.

"I volunteered for the job," Clara said dampingly, and made no secret of her lack of pleasure in it.

Nel skewered her with a blue gimlet eye and said, "I wonder why?" Clara ignored this mischievous statement.

Lady Marguerite was paying no heed to these few remarks. She looked preoccupied. "Did you go to Scotland after the Bellingham's party, Miss Christopher?" she asked, with still that strange, almost gloating look.

"Yes, I did. How did you know that?"

"Ben mentioned it. He happened to go north himself a little later and said he had just missed someone from the Bellinghams'." She turned to Nel and said, "I have figured out why you found Miss Christopher's manner toward Ben strange. It was his great pleasure in seeing her again that accounts for it. You mistook the direction of the familiarity."

The Incomparable did not condescend to reply to this remark. With a smirk and a steely eye she turned to Marguerite, showing Clara a broad view of her back. "What do you think of Oglethorpe?" she asked.

Knowing that he was Clara's cousin, she replied, "He seems very nice."

A trill of laughter greeted this. "What a quiz he is! I cannot think what your cousin sees in him. She is no great shakes herself, but she could surely do better than Oggie."

Clara said coldly, "That was not the impression you gave this afternoon when you were with him. You seemed quite infatuated."

"Oh I was just pestering Benjie. He is a fiend of jealousy—you've no idea. I don't know why men are all so jealous."

"Sure it wasn't Prissie you were pestering?" Lady Marguerite asked with a sapient look.

"I can't help it if she took a snit. As if I'd look twice at him, with Benjie in the same room. But she was always a ninny."

Yet Nel had looked more than twice at him, with Ben not only in the same room, but right at her elbow. In her broad dealings with society, Clara had encountered many specimens of human nature, but it had not fallen to her lot before to meet anyone quite like Miss Muldoon. Clara had long ago discarded the old myth that homely girls were better-natured. They were more likely to be bad-natured, from jealousy or lack of attention or just plain anger at being unattractive. Pretty girls, especially if they were heiresses, as Miss Muldoon was, were generally agreeable. They had more than their share of suitors and attention. They were silly and a little vain sometimes, but not composed of pure spite.

Miss Muldoon, with a fortune at her back and the face of an angel, was pure mischief from the top of her golden curls to the toe of her dainty blue slippers. And she had taken on the job of chaperoning this minx all during the busy nuptial party. It would not do to begin by being rude to her, as she was sorely tempted to be. Clara braced herself to be agreeable and complimented Nel on her gown. It was not the lutestring of the afternoon, but a silk empress style in a similar shade of blue.

Miss Muldoon thought it over a moment and decided this line of talk was acceptable. "It is from Mademoiselle du Puis in London," she said, with great condescension. "She makes all my gowns. Of course my riding habits are made by an English modiste. The French cannot make a decent riding habit. They refuse to allow breathing space, and when one really rides, one needs that. Do you ride, Miss Christopher?"

"A little," Clara answered. She doubted at the moment whether what she did on a horse was really riding.

Miss Muldoon regaled them with a tale of a hunt she had participated in, in which she got bloodied, was given the tail, and generally distinguished herself above all: both by her English-cut habit of scarlet and her superior riding over field, hedge, and water.

"How nice," Clara smiled.

"You must have improved tremendously," Lady Marguerite said tartly. "You fell off your mount the one time I hunted with you, and that was less than a year ago."

"Benjie has been giving me lessons. He is a great hunter, and says I must learn if I . . . He says I must learn," she finished archly, content that she had let them know her meaning without saying it.

"Certainly you must if you don't want to break a leg," Lady Marguerite said. With an impish smile she added, "If you lamed any of Ben's nags, he'd have both you and it shot."

It seemed a long while before the gentlemen began straggling into the saloon, but when they did, Miss Muldoon came to sharp attention. Allingcote was a step ahead of the others. After a quick look around the room, he headed straightway to the three ladies in the corner. He seemed happy or perhaps just relieved, to see peace reigning there. But when first his sister, then Clara, rose quickly and dashed off, he assumed Nel was not finding any favor with the ladies.

Clara claimed she must speak to Lady Lucker and darted toward her. After exchanging a few idle remarks with her hostess to lend credence to her excuse, she joined Lady Marguerite by the grate. "Ugh," the young lady said bluntly. "If Ben brings that witch home as his wife, I shall leave the house."

"She is rather—trying," Clara said, in a certain tone that conveyed more than mere words. "Is he likely to, do you think?"

"It begins to look that way, but of course Nel is a dreadful liar. Perhaps she believes her own stories, who knows? In any case, she would not be trying to make *me* jealous of my own brother, so unless *you* are the butt of her jibes, Miss Christopher, I don't see the point of her stories."

"I cannot think they were directed at me, a mere acquaintance," Clara said quickly.

Marguerite turned her sharp eyes, so like Lady Lucker's, on her new friend. "She is ravishingly beautiful, of course, and that would count with Ben."

"She is remarkably pretty, certainly. Is she an old friend of the family?" Clara asked, in a voice of the utmost civility and indifference.

"Not exactly. Her uncle, Lord Anglin, was a close friend of my papa, and since she's been staying with Anglin the past two years, we've seen more of her than is entirely comfortable. She's only seventeen. Till she left school last year she was not considered eligible. Since then, Ben has seen a good deal of her. That he spent a whole week there looks ominous. And especially his choosing to hide it from me and Mama. He knows a match in that quarter would be unpopular with us."

Marguerite slid a look to the corner of the room just in time to see Nel lay a fluttering white hand on her brother's arm and smile up with a languishing look. Clara followed the direction of her gaze and saw Allingcote lay his hand on top of Nel's.

"If she doesn't nab him, it won't be for lack of trying," Marguerite scowled.

While they chatted, Clara fell to wondering why Miss Muldoon should contemplate running away from Allingcote in the dead of night if she was in love with him. A frown creased her brow, and a little later she risked another glance toward the corner. Allingcote was gazing steadily at her. From the still position of his body, it seemed he might have been staring for a little while. He smiled across the room, and Clara found, when she glanced away, that she had forgotten to observe Nel. She also noticed that her heart was beating faster, and soon she noticed that Lady Marguerite was looking at her with a very lively interest.

"The merest of acquaintances, are you?" she teased. "I am surprised you admit to knowing him at all. He said you are very cautious, but I think you are very sly, Miss Christopher. May I call you Clara? And I hope you will call me Maggie."

Clara blushed up to her eyes. "Certainly you may, but I don't know what you mean by calling me sly."

"Don't you, Clara? You can trust me. I am as silent as a giraffe when I want to be. I shan't say a word. And to show you how much I approve, I'll spell Ben from the beauty so he can come to you. I shall let on I want to talk to her. Now that, you must own, is a great sacrifice on my part."

Clara was surprised at the rushing forward of intimacies between Ben's sister and herself. She would not have presumed to use Marguerite's first name for another week at least. Marguerite rose and tipped across the room to make a few joking comments to her brother. In a gratifyingly short space of time, Allingcote rose and crossed the room to possess the chair left vacant by his sister.

"Deserter!" he challenged. "Why did you and Maggie shab off on me?"

Clara examined him with great curiosity. He was as well as saying he didn't care for Miss Muldoon's company, yet he had, surely not under constraint, spent the past week with her. Had indeed spent some considerable part of the past year with her, teaching her to ride.

"Speechless with guilt, I see," he went on, but when he glanced back to Miss Muldoon's corner, he cast a fond smile on Nel, and she waved back merrily. "She's fagged from the trip and other exertions," he said. "I'd like her to get to bed early tonight, if you don't mind leaving this party soon—in an hour or so, if that's all right?"

"I've been under more exertion than I am accustomed to myself lately. I shan't mind leaving early. Not that I'll sleep."

Allingcote studied her face and a frown formed between his eyes. "I don't see why you let Charity run you like a servant," he said gruffly. Clara blinked in surprise, and he continued in a lighter tone. "You are not standing high enough on your dignity as the groom's cousin, Miss Christopher. But you may sleep tonight without a single fear—or hope—of finding Nel's bed empty in the morning. We have had a heart-to-heart talk, and I've convinced her."

"Of what?"

"Of there being no point in her leaving tonight."

"Tonight, but tomorrow I shall have the pleasure of a sleepless night?"

"One day at a time. That's the way to proceed in these perilous ventures. Tomorrow night, Maggie will take your place." He extended a hand and patted her arm in an avuncular manner. It was a mere nothing, but Clara felt his touch clear up to her head and down to her toes. "You busy servants need your rest. You'll be placing Max the pincher between two appetizing morsels of femininity if you don't have your wits about you." Glancing around, he added, "That'd be between yourself and Nel. The party is noticeably lacking in pulchritude."

A compliment placing her in tandem with Nel Muldoon found little favor. Clara said, "Does Maggie—your sister—know of this arrangement?"

"We call her Maggie, *en famille.* I am happy she has asked you to do the same. I know the cautious Miss Christopher would not have advanced so fast without a hint. I haven't told her yet, but she always does what I ask, and sometimes what I want even without being asked. A darling sister, don't you think?" he asked with a lazy smile that set Clara to wondering what had passed between brother and sister.

She also noticed that he used that "darling" in a careless way. Perhaps it did not signify, his calling Nel a darling. Clara cleared her throat and expressed some mild approbation of Maggie.

Allingcote shook his head. "I used to think calmness was your outstanding characteristic, Miss Christopher, but I begin to see caution runs it a close second."

"Hardly an attribute you will regret in the present circumstances, when your friend requires such a deal of it," she replied blandly.

"Not an attribute to be despised at any time. Or almost any time," he added deliberately. His dark eyes, studying her, seemed to suggest some particular significance in the present moment. "But I think I prefer your calmness."

It was not easy to remain calm under his penetrating gaze, while a little smile hovered on his lips. "Ah, the tea tray," Clara said, happy for a diversion.

"Saved by the pot," he laughed. "Shall I get you a cup? A little milk and no sugar, right?"

Clara looked at him in fascination. "Are you a mind reader, Lord Allingcote?"

"No, ma'am. I wish I were, but I have often gotten tea for you in the past, and I am blessed, you recall, with an excellent memory."

"But so long ago!"

"It has seemed *ages* to me," he said softly, leaning his head closer to hers and looking at her with such a meaningful expression that her poor mind went reeling.

She thought if this intimate behavior was kept up, her calmness would vanish, but it did not continue. When Allingcote returned with her tea, actually with more milk than she liked, he settled down to some amusing but innocuous discussion of the wedding, the family—his own and Prissie's—and after a quarter of an hour he rose and excused himself to converse with others, just as he should. A little later he was required to rescue Nel from the advances of an elderly roué at whom she had been rolling her eyes.

Clara had been watching Nel's new flirtation with some interest, wondering how long it would take Allingcote to become incensed with it. He seemed more amused than angry at first. Clara did not find him a fiend of jealousy, but eventually he did make his way toward Nel. As the hour was a little more than up by this time, he brought Nel toward Clara. "Ready?" was all he said. She nodded, and the three of them left the room together.

Chapter Seven

There was no hope of congenial conversation in the carriage with Miss Muldoon on the way to the inn. She had only one interest: herself. She complained at having to leave the house, complained of the cold, of the dullness of the party just left, and prophesied unaired beds and lumpy mattresses at the inn.

"You're overly tired," Allingcote said forgivingly.

"I am not tired," she declared, and in a final fit of pique added, "at least I trust you will not register me as Nellie Muldoon."

They were just descending from the carriage, and Clara frowned at her charge, wondering what she meant.

"Who are you tonight, Nel?" Ben asked. "Mrs. Siddons, perhaps. Or is it a princess in disguise?"

"Don't be silly. I'm much too young and pretty to be Sarah Siddons. I shall be Lady Arabella de Coverley, and Miss Christopher will be my abigail."

"I expect Miss Christopher will have something to say about that," he said, and strode to the desk. "Miss Nel Muldoon," he said in a loud voice.

Nel regarded him with loathing and said, "Come along, Miss Christopher."

The interaction between Allingcote and Nel seemed less lover-like at every moment, and Clara's curiosity mounted higher. "Why do you call yourself Lady Arabella?" she asked.

"Nellie doesn't suit me. It is a name for a dairymaid, or a servant girl. My name is actually Helena, but people call me Nel in spite, for they know I hate it. Arabella suits me better."

Clara mentioned that she doubted there was any spite in it. Nel was a common nickname for Helen, but the common quality of it was exactly what irked the beauty. Nel flounced her shoulders and went on to mention a few other names she considered worthy of herself and occasionally used: Cecilia, Aurora, Naomi. Clara concluded this was a childish game invented to give herself airs and added a few likely ones that Nel had omitted. Thus occupied, she did not observe that Lord Allingcote was for some few minutes in conversation with the proprietor. She had no way of hearing the questions he was putting to the man, or what answers he received.

"Has a young dark-haired gentleman been asking for Miss Muldoon?"

"No, sir. No one has inquired for her at all."

"If he shows up I would like to be notified at once," Allingcote said. "No matter what hour, wake me any hour of the night. And—ah—no need to let the gentleman know I have been inquiring." He slipped a golden boy into the innkeeper's hand and received a hearty, "Right you are, milord," in reply, before returning to the ladies.

They were no sooner shown into their rooms— fine, spacious, clean rooms—than Nel began finding fault. The bed was too hard. She couldn't sleep on a hard bed. Clara offered to change, but hers was too soft. The rooms were cold and drafty with a dozen wrong things, but when all her complaints were uttered, Ben said flatly, "They're the last empty rooms in the place. It's here or the stable, Nel."

"Let me have your room, and you can have mine. I wager your bed has a good mattress."

"A charming idea, but it has slipped your notice that your room adjoins Miss Christopher's, without benefit of door. Just the curtained archway, you see."

"Oh poo!" She tossed her curls, flung her bonnet on the dresser, and said. "You shan't care about that."

"Miss Christopher shall, however. Unlike yourself, *she* has some sense of propriety. Go to bed now," he said, and turned toward the door.

"I'm hungry," she called after him.

"It is not two hours since dinner."

"Dinner was horrid. I didn't eat a bite. I'm starved. I can never sleep when I'm hungry."

"Try, Nel."

"A bowl of gruel would not take long," Clara suggested, to have done with it. "We could have it sent up."

Miss Muldoon stared at her as if she were insane. "Gruel!"

"An excellent notion," Allingcote grinned. "I shall ask to have a bowl of gruel sent up."

"I don't want gruel. I hate gruel."

"You are not getting belowstairs tonight, Nel," he said firmly. "I'll order gruel if you think you'll expire before morning, but it comes up. You don't go down."

Nel threw off her pelisse and assumed a Stoic attitude. "In that case, I'll go hungry." She walked to the door and held it wide for Allingcote to leave.

"That'll teach me," he said, chucking her chin, and with an apologetic shrug back at Clara, he left. Nel tried a little more wheedling on Clara, whom she judged to be made of softer stuff. Taking her cue from Allingcote, Clara was adamant and the subject was finally dropped.

Nel next tried her hand at turning Clara into an abigail, and again she was thwarted. Clara limited her services to unfastening the back of the girl's gown. Even when Nel kicked her good blue silk into a heap on the floor and left it there, Clara quelled the urge to pick it up. She suggested Nel do it, but did not insist.

"If you wish to look as though you had slept in it, there was no point in taking it off" is all she said.

"I am not accustomed to doing servants' work" was the lofty rejoinder.

"No more am I," Clara retorted, and went through the curtain before she gave in to the impulse to pick the beautiful gown up. She had noticed that Nel's lingerie was of the finest, too, all embroidered in silk. It seemed woefully unfair that one lady should have so much, especially when she was so unappreciative.

73

She peeked once through the curtain at the gown on the floor. Such a beautiful gown! But she would not knuckle under to Nel Muldoon.

Clara was soon in bed with her candle extinguished. Her own gold taffeta hung carefully on a hanger. She was tired, but in a strange room, sleep did not come easily. She had ample time to wonder why Miss Muldoon, a troublesome heiress, traveled without an abigail, and why she was so determined to get downstairs. Escape could not have been her aim. She did not mind if Allingcote went with her. Nor was hunger the reason. She refused food in her room. Was it only one last chance to find someone to flirt with, to make Ben jealous? But he hadn't seemed so very jealous.

She listened for sounds of escape in the adjoining room, but heard only silence. A little later, she heard the long breaths of sleep. Doubting that Nel was clever enough to simulate sleep so well, she relaxed. Before she slept herself, she indulged in a long recall of that interesting day. Allingcote's coming and seeming so happy to see her again. His sharp recollection of their former meeting in all its details, his renewed attentions, and Maggie's strange expression when she asked if it had been at Bellingham's that she met Ben. Obviously Ben had spoken of that party at home. Finally she thought how remarkably strange it was that she should be sleeping in the same inn as he, with only Nel Muldoon between them. On this symbolic thought, she slept.

Chapter Eight

When Clara opened her eyes to an unfamiliar set of walls and draperies in the morning, she was momentarily confused. No sense of panic accompanied her confusion. She merely had to lie still a moment and think: where am I staying this week? This was not her room at Branelea—ah yes, the wedding, Allingcote, the inn—Miss Muldoon! Clara leapt from bed and ducked through the curtained arch to ascertain that Miss Muldoon still slept, as indeed she did.

If only the chit could remain a Sleeping Beauty! In repose, she looked young and vulnerable, with her tousled curls spread over the pillow, and her rosebud lips partly open. She slept deeply, and as a glance at her watch told Clara it was only seven o'clock, she decided she, too, would return to bed for an hour. She didn't expect to sleep, but to lie and anticipate that in an hour or so, she would be having breakfast with Allingcote.

Before she had mentally had more than a bite of toast, for food figured very sparingly in this imaginary breakfast, she was back to sleep. And before much longer, Miss Muldoon's blue eyes fluttered open. She lay still a moment listening. When she heard only silence beyond the curtain, she sat up, swung her legs out of bed, snatched her crumpled gown from the floor, and scrambled into it. Unable to fasten the back buttons, she threw a shawl over her shoulders and went tiptoeing down the stairs, peering about to left and right like a spy.

"Good morning, Lady Arabella," a cheerful voice called from an open doorway, and Lord Allingcote stood quizzing her. "I trust you slept well? Forgot to bring your hairbrush, did you? Never mind, Miss Christopher will be kind enough to lend you hers."

Nel assumed a dramatic pose and declaimed, "I hate you with all my heart, Benjamin Davenport!"

A passing servant girl stopped to goggle at such interesting goings-on at an inn whose liveliest customer was usually a drunken traveler. "Breakfast for two, miss, if you please," Allingcote told the servant, and ushered Nel into a private parlor.

"At least let us hide your shameful dishevelment in here if you don't mean to tidy up," he said.

When they were alone, her melodramatic manner vanished, and she took a chair, accepted coffee that he poured from the pot on the table, and sipped it calmly. "He hasn't arrived yet," Allingcote said. "You missed your beauty sleep to no avail. Did you sleep in that gown, by the by? He won't like to see you looking so slovenly."

"He will be *aux anges* to see me looking any way at all," she replied smugly.

In a short while food was brought by the highly

interested serving girl. Hard at her heels came Miss Christopher, in the wildest disarray that she had ever appeared in in public. Her usually neat coil of hair had slipped from its hastily arranged roll, and a curl fell over her ear. Like Nel, her gown's undone buttons were covered by her shawl. She came pelting into the parlor, and upon seeing Allingcote, she cried, "She's gone, Ben! I have let her escape. Whatever are we to do?" In her state of agitation, she didn't notice she had called Allingcote, Ben.

The servant dropped a plate of hot buns on to the table in excitement. One fell unobserved into Allingcote's cup. As the words left Clara's mouth, she spotted Nel sitting at the other end of the table, beyond her view from the doorway. Clara stopped dead.

"Good morning, Miss Christopher," Allingcote said, rising and bowing. "Make that breakfast for three, miss," he added aside to the servant. "And a fresh cup of coffee for me, if you will be so kind. My bread seems to have drunk mine," he said, peering into his cup. The servant just stood, her curious gaze running from one of the group to the other.

"You must not fear that your kitten has run off, Miss Christopher," he said to Clara. "You really should have closed the lid of its basket, but no matter. We shall have a look about the roads as soon as we've eaten." He walked toward Clara and held her chair for her, just sliding his eyes in an admonishing way toward the staring servant, to explain this seemingly irrelevant talk of kittens.

"Ye didn't bring no kitten with yez," the servant said.

Nel was charmed with this chance for a little play-acting, and joined in, her eyes sparkling with pleasure. "Hush!" she said, looking over her shoulder with awful caution. "It is a very special kitten. It was necessary to conceal it. The French are after it, you see."

"What would they Frenchies be wanting a cat for?"

"It's Queen Charlotte's cat, and they want to hold it for ransom," the inventive Nel explained.

From her smiles, Allingcote knew she was about to begin a long story. "But not a word of it below-stairs, mind!" he said to the servant who continued regarding them all with the deepest mistrust. "May we have our coffee now, please?" he said, to be rid of her.

She poured the coffee and left, looking over her shoulder as if she expected to receive a knife in the back.

"What fun!" Nel chirped when they were alone. "When she comes back, I shall tell her there is a hundred-guineas reward for the recovery of the kitten. She will have every soul in the place out scouring the roads."

"What a pleasant idea, with the balmy December breezes blowing," Clara said, lifting an eyebrow at Miss Muldoon. Noticing Nel's state of undress, for her gown was beginning to slip from her shoulder, she added, "You look a fright, Miss Muldoon. You should have tidied up before coming downstairs."

"So should you," Nel replied triumphantly.

Clara's hand flew to her hair. She brushed back

the loose curl with one hand, clutching her shawl with the other, while her eyes flew to Allingcote. He was regarding her with amusement.

"Now you have placed me in an untenable position, Nel," he said. "I can hardly praise Miss Christopher's charming dishabille when I have just been giving you the devil for yours. Might I suggest you both take a moment to tidy up? There is a mirror and a washbasin behind that curtain. You go first, Nel. Do you have a comb?"

"No."

"I have one in my reticule," Clara offered, but she had some difficulty extracting it while still trying to hold herself together, so she handed Nel the bag.

Nel, less bashful, pulled off her shawl and demanded Miss Christopher do up her back buttons before she leave. Such a hand-demanding chore as this was beyond Clara, however, and it was Allingcote who struggled with a dozen pea-sized buttons much too small for his fingers.

"My reputation wouldn't be worth a Birmingham farthing if anyone were to see me at this moment," he declared ruefully. "Two half-dressed ladies in a private parlor with me at eight o'clock in the morning. I shall think twice before jumping to conclusions another time."

"I daresay you'd be happy enough to be considered so dashing," Nel said pertly, and ducked behind the curtain.

"You neglect to mention the ladies' reputations would suffer even more," Clara pointed out. She attempted an air of dignity, but her cheeks were flushed with embarrassment.

"There is a tried-and-true way to redeem a lady's reputation, Miss Christopher," he said, laughter lurking in his eyes, and a smile that he tried to conceal hovering about his lips.

"I know of no simple way for one gentleman to redeem two ladies' reputations simultaneously."

"We could always adopt her," he said, leaning closer and speaking in a low voice. He made no effort now to conceal his smile.

"I would as lief adopt a panther! And that servant knows perfectly well there is something amiss here, too. Did you see the way she stared?"

"I daresay most ladies dress before coming down to breakfast."

Clara clutched at her slipping gown.

"You'll choke yourself, Clara, if you pull that any tighter about your neck." She gave him a conscious, startled look, at hearing him address her so familiarly. Allingcote didn't explain or apologize his use of her first name, but continued speaking calmly. "I promise you I haven't seen a thing, despite the most strenuous looking. No, I was joking! Do relax. You are not your usual calm self this morning. I intercepted her at the bottom of the stairs. She hasn't had time to do anything. I assume, by the way, that you managed to get a few winks of sleep? I am happy for it."

"I was awake at seven. She was sound asleep. I didn't mean to doze off again . . ."

"Don't apologize. I am responsible for Nel."

"But why did she do it? Is she trying to run away?"

"No, not yet."

Before more could be said, Nel was back. "How did you think to bring your reticule in all your rush?" she asked Clara.

"I have my money in it. I couldn't leave it behind."

"You only have a guinea and a few shillings."

"Seven, unless you've helped yourself to a couple," Allingcote said. "Nice of you to check and see they were safe, Nel," he said with a sardonic smile. "Better count them," he added aside to Clara, who steeled herself not to do just that.

Nel sat down, unoffended, and sipped her coffee. Clara rose and went behind the curtain to view what a disgraceful sight she had presented to Lord Allingcote. She was ready to strangle Nel Muldoon—and to think that bold creature had gone rifling through her reticule, counting her money. She got her buttons done up with no great difficulty and wore a face worthy of a Methodist spinster when she returned to the table. She was determined to bring some semblance of decorum to this meal that had begun so badly.

"Now that looks more like my Miss Christopher," Ben said, regarding her. Clara foresaw considerable difficulty in her task, if this was the way he meant to carry on.

"Why do you call her *your* Miss Christopher?" Nel demanded at once. "You hardly know her."

"We are old friends," he replied.

"Miss Christopher told me you are hardly even acquaintances," Nel said, with a suspicious glance at Clara.

"Ah, well one never contradicts a lady, but for the merest of acquaintances, we are fast becoming good friends. Sharing a mutual problem—you, Nel—will often have that effect."

"You still should not call her your Miss Christopher, Benjie. It sounds so very odd, as though you are sweet on her or something," Nel persisted, seeing that she was upsetting Clara.

"I stand corrected," Ben said, with a bow of the head toward Miss Muldoon. "We are fortunate to have such a pillar of propriety to instruct us, Miss Christopher, are we not?"

"I am very sharp about some things," Nel rattled on. "Especially about romance. You should not be making up to Miss Christopher. Quite apart from the fact that you might inadvertently raise expectations in someone like her, you are supposed to be escorting *me*."

Clara sat, speechless, but Ben, after one angry glare, decided to ignore it. "Escorting you is certainly a full-time job," he said through thin lips. The servant appeared with their food, and he added, "Might I suggest you limit your sharp wits to eating your breakfast as quickly as possible."

Nel entered into a monologue on the ransom of the imaginary lost kitten till the servant left. Then she turned her attention to her food and the meal passed without further unpleasantness.

Clara was to return to Branelea immediately after breakfast. She risked letting Nel go abovestairs alone to her room while she gently hinted that Lady Lucker hoped Allingcote would keep Nel busy, preferably away from the house. She was surprised to see that he was actually angry at her hint. He tried to hide it, but the fact was he was hurt and angry that Miss Muldoon should be treated like the interfering, bad-natured, uninvited guest she was.

"Very well, I'll keep her away," he said stiffly. "Take her out for a drive in the nice December frost. She'll likely catch pneumonia, which will please you all no end. It seems to me Nel is not the only one who is a little spoiled. Prissie could do with a good shaking as well."

"It is Prissie's home, and Prissie's wedding. Surely at this time she deserves some consideration. Miss Muldoon was not invited, after all."

"Nel receives very few invitations anywhere there is another female to be jealous of her, and they all are."

His sense of injury on Nel's behalf did nothing to soften Clara's feelings toward the girl. "It is your partiality that makes you see jealousy as the only reason she is unwelcome. It is her general lack of manners rather that causes disgust."

"I don't apologize for her. She is not well behaved, but there is a reason for it. Nel was orphaned two years ago. She has not had a real home since she was fifteen."

"I was orphaned when I was twelve, and have not had a real home since that time. I did not consider it an excuse for boorish behavior. But then I was never either a beauty or an heiress. No doubt such advantages allow one to behave as ill as she pleases, and still be called a lady."

Allingcote looked startled at her snappish reply. "My excuse was poorly chosen," he said at once. "Certainly she has neither your amiable temperament nor your firmness of character."

Clara frowned, wondering if he was being satirical. He rushed on in an attempt to lighten the atmosphere with a joke. "Shall we blame it all on their— Nel's and Prissie's—youth, Miss Christopher? What *is* this younger generation coming to? I seem to recall Papa saying much the same thing to me fifteen years ago when I bought my first flowered waistcoat."

Nel came back, complaining that her hair was a mess, and she couldn't do a thing without her abigail, Tolkein.

"Why is your abigail not with you?" Clara inquired, for this matter had been puzzling her.

"She's got the measles. Imagine, at her age, getting the measles like a baby."

"How old is she?"

"She's ancient. Thirty or forty—maybe fifty."

"Somewhere in there between thirty and a hundred," Ben smiled, in an effort to hide Nel's petulance.

"It serves her right," Nel continued. "I'm glad she got them. If she hadn't, I never could have—" She came to a stop and looked at Ben with a guilty start.

"Shall we go?" he asked quickly. As it was clear Clara was not to be let in on the secret, she was determined to show no curiosity. She went upstairs for her pelisse, bonnet, and bandbox, and went with them to the carriage.

When they reached Branelea, Ben seemed quite determined to get not only himself but Nel as well into the house, and there was no way of preventing him. Once inside, his reason for entering was revealed as being relatively harmless. He wanted to discover from the occupants where he might take Nel to amuse her. Nel dashed upstairs to borrow Prissie's abigail to do her hair more fashionably. Lady Lucker, who was in the morning parlor with her husband, racked her brain to think of a destination several miles distant she might suggest to her nephew.

"There's a dandy museum at Aldershott," Sir James mentioned, as he got out his coin collection.

"What kind of museum?" Allingcote asked.

"Old Roman artifacts," Sir James said, his smile suggesting this was a rare treat.

"Oh."

"You'll like it," Sir James insisted, and taking up his box of bent pieces of metal, he went along into his study.

Lady Lucker tallied up the hour it would take to go to Aldershott, the hour spent there, the hour to return, and seconded the plan vigorously. "The very thing. I shall just dash up and see if Miss Muldoon has got what she needs." She left to try to conceal from Prissie the fact that Nel was in the house at all.

Ben, alone now with Clara, turned a hopeful eye

to her. "I wonder if Sir James would like to take Nel to the museum."

"I shouldn't think so. He doesn't go out much in this weather."

"Why should he escape Nel entirely?"

"Why shouldn't he? She's not his problem."

"In these times of natural disaster, every man should be willing to do his duty. Nel is a one-woman disaster, wouldn't you say?"

"I would, but she's not his woman. She's yours."

"Only in a very restricted sense is she mine. She is my responsibility for the time being. And it seems I am stuck with her, to bear the burden alone. What will you do while we're gone?"

"I have plenty to keep me busy."

"Auntie will see to that. Well, work hard and get your jobs done. I shall take up my burden and leave, but I give you fair warning, when I get back, I expect your company to help me explore that island of ours." He bowed gracefully and left.

While he awaited Nel in the hall, Clara stood a moment in perplexity. After sticking up for Nel and trying to excuse her behavior, Allingcote turned around and admitted she was a disaster. He tried to avoid taking her out and seemed bent on continuing his interrupted flirtation with herself. He would find little opportunity to do it, she feared. She had a million things to do, and she set about doing them without wasting more time thinking about Lord Allingcote.

The hours till luncheon passed busily, even hectically, for Clara and Lady Lucker, working on the housing, feeding, and entertainment of the guests.

More arrivals came from afar, including Mr. Herbert Ormond, a cousin of Clara's, at whose family home she had once lived for four months. There had initially been a little constraint between them. When two young people of the opposite sex and marrying age are thrown together, they dare not be too friendly in case one or the other begins to form ideas. But as soon as it was discovered that Herbert must marry money and Miss Christopher had none, they could relax their formality and become friends. With no fear or hope of romance to inhibit the friendship, they had been meeting irregularly at various family reunions, always with pleasure on both sides.

Herbert and others had to be shown to their rooms. Wine and biscuits were served, newly arrived gifts were scrutinized and placed on display, and the guests were taken to admire them. Clara found much pleasure in all the busyness of the day, and also in the company of Lady Marguerite, who was becoming a friend as best she could at this eventful time. The young ladies would no sooner begin a conversation than they would be interrupted, but the frequent return of Maggie to her side made Clara realize that a definite effort was being made at friendship.

Clara still had the large task of arranging the seating of the wedding party at three tables, but not a moment to see to it. Before it seemed possible, luncheon was upon them, and Allingcote and Nel returned at the last possible moment before it was served. Again their places were at the far end of the table from Prissie and Oglethorpe. On this occasion the precaution proved unnecessary. Nel discovered a more interesting flirt in Herbert Ormond. He was a tall, fairly handsome gentleman with easy manners. Clara wished she had foreseen this possibility and placed him at Nel's side. He sat directly across from her, however, which was perhaps even better. It gave them an unimpeded view of each other. Herbert was clearly knocked off his pins at her beauty and hid it so little that Nel spent her time smiling at him, and hadn't a moment to pester Prissie.

Clara was happy for this new development, till she noticed that Lord Allingcote was watching the duo with a wary eye. It was the eye of a man who had more than a duty toward Nel. In fact, it was very like the eye of a lover.

Chapter Nine

After luncheon, the party assembled in the gold saloon. Herbert Ormond went immediately to Clara's side and began talking with her about the old times. Nel and Allingcote were seated not far from them.

"Have you seen old Sydenham lately?" Ormond asked, laughing at some private joke.

"He was at my aunt's wedding, forgetful as ever, and very nearly shoved me into the wedding carriage."

"I wager you put him up to it! A ship leaving for Greece would be a wicked temptation to one of your proclivities. Marven would not have minded," he said, naming the groom. "I daresay your aunt was not amused. I wanted to attend the wedding, but was away on business. I was especially sorry to miss the chance of seeing you, Clara. How did it go?"

"It was a small do, but very *haut ton*. And I missed seeing you at Cousin Caroline's coming-out ball, for I was gone to Devon and could not go all the way to London only for a ball."

"Some evil genie has been keeping us apart, Clara,

but at least we both managed to make it to this one. We must not lose touch again. It wouldn't hurt you to drop me a line occasionally. You get about and see everyone; you should keep me posted."

"Any letter of mine would not be worth the frank," she said dismissingly.

"Don't let that be your excuse! I would gladly pay to hear from you." Ormond noticed that Allingcote was inclining an ear in their direction and lowered his voice to ask what he might get Prissie for a gift.

Discreet inquiries as to what price they were discussing settled in her mind that the crystal compote dish on the list, and not yet received, was the very thing. She was able to tell him not only the shop, but also the shelf, from having often had it pointed out by Lady Lucker as a cherished item. Its cost was beyond Clara's means. She had to settle for wineglasses. When the gift business was settled, they sat back and Ormond said in his normal voice, "Why don't you come to the village with me, Clara? You are the very one to help me out."

"I cannot get away this afternoon," she said, shaking her head.

"It won't take more than an hour. You can give me an hour, surely. You did not used to be so stingy with your time."

"Really I don't think I can, much as I should like to. But I promise you an uninterrupted hour before you leave, Herbert."

Nel could not like to see a beau being attentive to another lady and bounced over to them. "Where is it you want to go, Mr. Ormond?"

"I must go to the village to get Prissie a gift."

"I'll go with you," she offered at once. "I love shopping. I haven't been in a single shop in the village, just driven past them a few times."

"I don't think that's a good idea, Miss Muldoon," Clara said, with a questioning look at Allingcote. There had been some talk of Anglin's not liking Nel to visit the shops, but more than this, it posed a danger of escape, while Nel was with an escort who was unaware of her intentions.

Allingcote's reply surprised her. "I see no harm in it. It will amuse Nel. Mind you, Mr. Ormond, when you escort such an Incomparable as Miss Muldoon, every precaution must be taken to protect her from the bucks. You will find a raft of them tagging at your heels."

Nel smiled in perfect contentment, but even more glory was in store for her. "The custom is to hold her very firmly by the arm at all times, and give a heavy set-down to any gent who becomes bothersome."

"I trust I am not about to become involved in a duel?" Ormond asked jokingly.

"With Miss Muldoon, there is no saying."

When the pair went for their coats, Clara asked Allingcote whether it was wise to let Nel go. "She would enjoy it, and I don't see what could happen in broad daylight," he replied. "If you wish to give Ormond a more direct hint, by all means, do so."

"It would come better from you."

"I thought as you are on such *intimate* terms with the gentleman . . ." His voice had thinned to sarcasm.

Clara felt a needle of irritation at his tone. A gentleman whose behavior was so irregular as Allingcote's had no right to sarcasm about another man, but from habit she damped down her irritation and said blandly, "Perhaps you're right. After her stunt this morning, it won't do to take any chances. If you hadn't met her downstairs, there is no saying what she might have done."

Ormond was ready before Nel, and Clara took the opportunity to warn him. She invented a tale that Nel had recently run away from school, and they feared she might bolt again. Really it was necessary to take a little extra precaution.

"I can't think of a more delightful way of spending an afternoon, unless it would be to hold on to you as well, Clara," he replied gallantly.

Allingcote's eyes narrowed a fraction as he looked from one to the other in a close way. Nel returned, and the shoppers left, with a nod over Ormond's shoulder as he took hold of Nel's arm, apparently bent on following his instructions quite literally.

"Have I done something gauche?" Allingcote asked, when the door closed behind them.

"I don't know about gauche, but I hope you haven't done something foolish."

"What I am asking you, in no clear way I fear, is whether Mr. Ormond is your beau? Is that why you did not wish Nel to go with him?"

"Mr. Ormond is my cousin and good friend. If he were a beau, I should not look in Miss Muldoon's direction for competition I promise you," Clara snipped. "Mr. Ormond is particularly sensible. And now I have an impertinent question for you, my lord.

I think it is time you told me the whole truth about Miss Muldoon. What spree, exactly, did her abigail's bout of measles allow her to indulge in?"

"I'm sorry if my question sounded impertinent to you. I consider it particularly pertinent myself. But about Nel, there is no point trying to keep it from you. The fact is, you guessed it yourself. She did run away, not from school, but from Anglin's house, when Miss Tolkein so thoughtlessly came down with measles. It was Nel's intention to go to London and go on the stage."

This struck Clara as entirely plausible. Indeed, Allingcote had even called her Mrs. Siddons, and the girl had a definite leaning toward playacting. "At least we shall know where to look for her if she slips the rein. It will be either Drury Lane or Covent Garden. She'll aim for the top and would probably make a good success of it, too. I shall treat this with confidence, as I know you don't wish it known. I must go now. Duty calls." Even while she made her remarks, Clara was thinking, why was the question pertinent?

"Did you get your jobs done this morning, as I asked you to?"

"A woman's work is never done, Allingcote."

"I hoped we might do something together this afternoon. Not necessarily explore the desert island, if you are becoming slightly bored with those two wilting palms. We might go for a drive—you could show me around the village."

"Was a morning in the balmy December breezes not sufficient for you? I fear you are a fresh-air fiend. I must confess I am not, particularly in winter."

"A keg of claret and another of sherry on the island then. Warm tropical sun and an occasional cooling draft from the loose windows. I'll bring along the words from 'The Maid of Lodi.' I have copied them out for you. 'Beautiful maid with chestnut hair . . .' You'll learn them in no time."

"That should be golden hair, if my poor memory serves."

His eyes flickered over her chestnut hair. "I have changed the words a little, to suit my own preference," he said.

"You must be required to change the shade frequently. At least once a week, I should think."

He studied her a moment before saying, "No, just once."

Clara refused to see any significance in all this pointed flirtation, and said briskly, "I have promised Lady Lucker to do the seating arrangements for the wedding dinner. I have just declined an outing with Mr. Ormond, and am really extremely busy."

"Let me help you," he suggested with pleasing promptness.

"That's not necessary. You go ahead with your walk; it is a small village. You will find your way about alone. In fact, why did you not go with Nel and Mr. Ormond?" Here was a mystery.

He tilted his head and gave her a mock frown of terrible severity. "It isn't really the fresh air I'm after, Miss Christopher. Where does this scheme of seating take place? In some quiet back parlor, I trust?"

It was in the little study that the seating cards

were put away, and it was to this spot that Clara led Allingcote. Her mind was seething with all his hints at wanting her company and preferring chestnut hair and pertinent questions about her having a beau. Even at the Bellinghams', he had not come so close to being explicit as this. She drew out the cards and three sheets of paper, outlining the seating arrangement of one large table and two smaller ones.

"What we wish to do is put the bride and groom and elevated guests at the largest table, and such minor nobodies as the provincial neighbors, myself, and Georgiana and Gertrude Snelley at the others, preferably with some mixing up of the two sides, Oglethorpe's and Prissie's. You can help, as the names and degree of eminence from her side are not so familiar to me. Now, where do we begin? Let us start with the large table. If you can find the cards for the bride and groom and immediate family, it will thin out the stack and make it more manageable."

Ben began laying the cards on the table before him, selecting certain ones and putting them aside. "Mama goes at the head table, I expect?"

"Certainly she does. The entire Allingcote family sits there."

"And Miss Christopher, you mentioned, goes at one of the lesser ones?"

"Below the salt," she said, with mock humility. "I am lucky to get a chair at all."

"If they don't let you have one, you are welcome to share mine. I like the idea immensely."

Clara turned a kindling eye on him. "Were you

used to be a gazetted flirt, Allingcote? My memory is impaired, of course, but I think I would remember if that were the case."

"Not gazetted. I am not listed in the official government journals. More of an undercover flirt. Oh dear, that sounds the very worst sort, does it not?" he replied with a teasing look. Clara frowned repressively. "I only meant—"

"I know what you meant," she said curtly, cutting his words off. "As my name is here, I expect there will be a chair for me."

He shrugged. "Too bad. How about Maximilian, the pincher? We'll give him a couple of well-corseted dowagers."

"No, no! All rich uncles are to have prime seats. Put him next to your mama at the head table, and tell her to watch out for his hands."

"He got the gold suite to himself. I say we stick him with Georgiana and Gertrude to pay for it."

"Do you want an uprising on your hands? The man is worth thousands, some small portion of which is hoped to trickle down to Oglethorpe."

"It's Prissie he ought to be pinching. No, I have a much better idea. Let him pinch you—no saying how much of his gold he might shower on you."

"I bruise easily. Pray put him between your mama and Maggie. And you can put yourself between Oglethorpe's mama and Lady Kiefer, Prissie's sister. But of course you know that."

"Worse, I know Emily, and her charming habit of not speaking when she's eating. Or any other time, actually. I wager she did no more than nod when

Kiefer popped the question. We'll put a good talker next to her. How about Mr. Ormond?"

"He is only a second cousin to Oglethorpe. I intended keeping him for myself. I expect I should give him to Miss Muldoon to play with, though, if it goes well with them this afternoon. Of course I could go on his other side—that would put me a little away from Nel," she said consideringly.

Allingcote drew an audible, impatient breath. "If you will look closely at these crooked cards I am laying out here—"

"Crooked! I spent hours ruling them out! They are straight as a die."

"More cheeseparing."

"What are you complaining about? Most of yours are store-bought. I have the homemade ones myself."

"The Countess Kiefer has a suspicious bulge here on the right side. Have you got some scissors?"

Clara found the scissors in a drawer and handed them to Allingcote, who carefully sheared a quarter of an inch off the card. "Next time you are making stationery, let me know. I have a steady hand, due to my clean living and high thinking. But it was really not your cutting ability we were discussing. If you look at this set of cards here, you will see, as well as their wobbly edges, that Lord Allingcote has been put at the head of one of the lesser tables. I prefer to be a big toad in a small puddle. Got quite a nick in my side, too, poor devil," he said, indicating the uneven edge of his card.

Clara glanced at it. "You shouldn't have. All you nobles were supposed to get the bought cards."

"And here at my left hand," he continued, "is Miss Christopher. She did an excellent job on her own card. I would prefer to put you on my right, but Miss Muldoon will have something to say about that."

"We are not much concerned with precedence at the smaller tables. There is not a title among us, and that includes Lord Allingcote's earldom," she said firmly.

"Grossly unfair! I shall put one of us elevated lords at each of the minor tables, to lend them a bit of ton. Myself at yours, and Sir Lawrence Malcolm at the other. He's almost a lord. A baronet will do well enough for Georgiana and Gertrude, whoever they may be."

"Sir James's unmarried cousins. They wear gray, and twitch their noses when they eat. They drink a deal of wine when no one is looking."

"Except Miss Christopher. I see you have spied out their vice. They must be invisible. I haven't seen them. Along with yourself, they seem to represent the very dregs of this prestigious affair, socially speaking that is. And it was still a dreadful thing to say, wasn't it? I am not usually so woolly-tongued."

"Yes, it was rude. I may run myself down as much as I please, but it is unbecoming in you to agree with me. It is not Lady Lucker's intention to mix the nobility and the hoi polloi. However eager you may be for Miss Muldoon's company, you will have to be deprived of it for an hour. I shall endeavor to seat her in such a way that you can see and admire her, if that will do."

"That is the very best way to appreciate Nel, but

it is not only her company I mean to procure. Auntie's objections to my plan of seating myself at your table will not be strenuous. It won't cost her a penny."

"You are not at all nice to speak so disrespectfully of your aunt."

"No more I am, but I am extremely pigheaded to make up for it. Now as a mere cousin of Oglethorpe, virtually hired help, you are not nice either to set your back against me. We sit at the lower table, but I'll throw in a concession for you. You can have Ormond on your other side. Will that do? You can commiserate together on all the times you have missed seeing each other. Poor planning on someone's part."

Clara noticed the sharp edge to his voice, which sounded delightfully like jealousy, and her spirits improved. "No, you had best give him to Miss Muldoon, tentatively at least. If she has not come to cuffs with him by the day of the wedding, we shall let it stand."

"Sure you can bear to part with him?" he asked, holding his card poised above Nel's.

"At such a time we must all make sacrifices for the sake of the party."

"How much of a sacrifice is it?" he asked, looking at the card and picking up the scissors to trim Ormond into a more proper shape.

"My heart was not entirely set on it. If I am to have a genuine peer of the realm on one side, anyone will do for the other. Ormond is heir to a barony, actually. I should not monopolize more than my share of nobility."

"I didn't know," he said, cutting the card smaller.

"Allingcote! Leave his name intact at least!" she exclaimed, as another piece fell from the card.

"The urge to cut him to shreds is strong, but with regard to Auntie's cardboard, I'll leave him in one piece beside Nel, where he can do no harm. Now, who would you like on your other side? Anyone under, say eighteen, and over fifty. With those two reservations you may have your pick."

"You are determined to do me out of any potential suitors, I see."

"Have you forgotten so soon I put myself beside you? How many suitors can you handle at one time?" he asked, moving his eyebrows playfully.

Clara was finding it hard to handle one, when it seemed his intention to flirt away the afternoon with her. "I think it will be Miss Muldoon who is handling you. Whatever about myself, I cannot think two will be beyond her powers. Give me Major Standby."

He shuffled through the stack and found the card. "A military man, eh? You'd best tell me a little about him before I let you have him. I don't want a dashing officer in a scarlet tunic to compete with."

"He's retired, sixty or seventy years old. He likes to talk about his wound while he's eating. It might be off-putting to any lady who has not heard it before. He was pinioned to a fence with an arrow in America, by a Cree Indian."

"Appetizing. Through the abdomen?"

"No, through the upper arm. With the least en-

100

couragement he can be induced to remove his jacket, roll up his shirt sleeve, and show the scar. It's purple."

"Sounds interesting."

"Yes, there is a whole epic that goes with it, and gets longer with each telling. He pulled the arrow out with his left hand, and went on to chase the scalp-hunter into the woods. He lost him."

"Hardly heroic. He couldn't see the Cree for the forest, I expect. Very well, Major Standby and his scar it is. If he's too shy to remove his jacket, I'll keep you entertained by showing you my scar. Nothing so glamorous as an Indian's arrow, I fear. I stuck an ice pick through my finger ten years ago, and still have the mark. It's not purple, or even pink. It's white. Right here," he said, holding out his left hand to her. Clara glanced at it, but was unimpressed with a white crescent a quarter of an inch long.

"It doesn't hold a candle to Major Standby's," she told him regretfully.

"It's worse than it looks. If you feel it, you will notice the skin is still uneven." He took her right hand and ran her fingers over the scar, which was barely perceptible to either sight or touch. His hand tightened over her fingers, and he held them a moment in complete silence.

Clara was overcome with a suffocating but quite delightful embarrassment. She knew she should object to such shocking flirtation as this, but had the feeling as well that something more extraordinary than holding hands was about to happen. She sat irresolute, then Ben let her fingers go and laughed. It was again that high, nervous laugh of their first meeting.

"Lucky I lived at all," he said. "I must get busy and compose an epic—or sonnet perhaps about it. I lost a whole teaspoon of blood. At least it looked like a teaspoonful on my handkerchief. It was certainly a visible spot at least. Your major is not the only hero around, you see. Good thing Nel is not here to point out to me he is not your major. Now, who goes next to him?"

His nervous babble came to a stop, and the moment was over. Clara turned briskly to business. She gave no encouragement to his many animadversions on those relatives from his side of the family. "You're a slave driver, Miss Christopher," he said in a teasing way when she had thrice called him to attention. "I am not hired help, you know. You should show me a little deference."

"I am not hired help either, and you, sir, are no help at all. In fact, the word hindrance comes to mind, but of course I shan't say it to Lady Lucker's nephew."

"She would take it sorely amiss if you did. She is trying to sweet-talk me into two dozen Wedgwood cups to go with the tea service I am giving Prissie. Till I come up to scratch, I am to be courted."

"The Countess Kiefer has been similarly hinted, and has capitulated. If a china tea service is as high as your benevolence goes, I shall tell you what I think of you."

"No, no. The tea set is silver, but don't let that pre-

102

vent you from speaking your mind. I would like to hear what you think of me."

She gave a saucy smile. "Would you? I cannot think what pleasure you should derive from hearing you are a pest and a nuisance, and a very sluggardly helper who is well paid at nothing an hour."

"Worthless, in fact. Without worth, or price. Priceless is another way of saying it. I am charmed that you think me priceless, Clara."

Clara stared at him in numb fascination. "You really ought to take up politics, Allingcote."

The job was finally done, and Clara had to leave as she was needed elsewhere.

"I have something I must do, too," Allingcote said. Before she went abovestairs, she saw him leave by the front door, wearing his greatcoat.

She was naturally curious to know where he was going, but did not ask. He said nothing, but waved and left. He bolted to the inn to inquire whether a certain gentleman had arrived yet, and to remind the proprietor to notify him at once if the man came.

Clara was not much help to Lady Lucker the rest of the afternoon. Her mind was too preoccupied with the interlude in the study, trying to decide whether it was mere flirtation, in which case she should not encourage it, or if it was something more. The word *suitor* had been used, but to counterbalance that, there was Nel Muldoon with her particular claims on Allingcote. With her mind in a turmoil, Clara threw out a magnificent piece of silver paper that could most certainly have been used to advantage again. Fortunately Lady Lucker did not come to know of the waste.

Chapter Ten

Herbert Ormond and Nel returned late in the afternoon, the former with no tales of attempted escape,
and the latter in high spirits. A large throng, grow-
ing larger by the minute, gathered in the gold saloon
before dinner. When Clara noticed out of the corner
of her eye that Nel was working her way toward
Prissie, she was alarmed. She watched, ready to intervene, but whatever passed between them, Prissie
actually smiled and talked to her old schoolmate for
quite five minutes without a single sign of pique.

Clara was prevented from discovering the subject
of their talk, for Lady Lucker, casting a wide, pleading eye at her, asked if she would just gather up a
tray of used glasses and get a servant to wash them
as they would be needed very soon for dinner. Clara
began attending to this in an unobtrusive manner
and soon noticed a black form at her shoulder.

"Can you use a hand?" Allingcote asked. "I am not
much good at drying, but will be happy to rinse these
out for you. They are to be used for dinner, I pre-
sume?" He smiled as he spoke, for of course not even

Lady Lucker would suggest that a guest wash the dishes.

"I take it Braemore also suffers a shortage of wine glasses, as you know the routine?"

"If it does, Mama has concealed it from me. I think you should hit Auntie up for an increase in your salary. She isn't actually poor, you know, and she's running you pretty hard."

"I do know it, but at such a time as this, with so many mouths to feed, it would be maladroit of me to dun her. There is that dreadful Maximilian taking *another* clean glass. Why does he not just ask for a refill?"

"He's ashamed to admit he's on his third. He hides the empties behind our potted palms—littering our favorite island. Shall I speak to him?"

"No!" she exclaimed in alarm, as Allingcote took a step toward him. Ben laughed openly and taking up a tray, began collecting a batch of used glasses himself, with no air of behaving badly.

Clara made a stop at the dining hall to confirm that Miss Muldoon was placed next to Herbert Ormond and to notice with a rueful smile that she herself was once again well removed from Allingcote. She wished he would come and rearrange the seating scheme, as he had that afternoon. During dinner, she was happy to see how well Nel and Ormond got on. She was surprised. Herbert was a good ten years older than the girl, and really she had always taken him for a sensible person. Several times she looked at the two of them, trying to figure it out. Though she did not notice it, Allingcote was as often regarding the direction of her intent gaze and wondering what this interest in Ormond denoted.

Some of the guests sang and played music after dinner. Clara remembered Ben had mentioned singing the "The Maid of Lodi," but he did not do so. Nor did Nel perform, but she was kept entertained and out of mischief with the concert. She was apparently satisfied with her place between Allingcote and Ormond, the two most handsome young gentlemen in the room, both of whom were at pains to amuse her with mild flirtations.

Clara felt piqued at having no other company herself than Major Standby and his scar. Since Nel was safely occupied with Ormond, she thought Ben might take up the empty chair beside her, but he made no move to do so. He knew it was empty; she saw him glance at it twice. Once he seemed to be pointing it out to Ormond, but neither of them was willing to leave Nel to the other.

Not till the concert was over was there any move in her direction, and then it was Ormond who strolled over and chatted for ten minutes about the most trivial of social nothings, and about Miss Muldoon. Clara was not to go to the inn that night. Maggie had been given the job, so it seemed Clara was not to have a word with Ben at all. She happened to be glancing in his direction when he and Nel rose to go for their coats, and he took a detour toward her.

"We haven't had a chance to chat all evening, Miss Christopher."

Not having a chance was a strange way of putting it. She was not about to let him off with that. "Kind

106

of you not to rob me of another opportunity to see Major Standby's scar," she said.

"I had to discover what sort of gentleman Mr. Ormond is, as I hope to use him as Nel's escort."

"My vouching for him was not sufficient?" she inquired coolly.

"Men behave differently with different ladies."

"So I have noticed."

He just laughed. "You are out of sorts. Get a good sleep," he said. "You are back on duty tomorrow night. I'll take Nel out in the morning. Perhaps Ormond will want to replace me in the afternoon. Have you got any jobs lined up for your helper?"

"If you refer to yourself, I cannot afford a lazy earl."

"We have agreed I am beyond price. It is only the perquisites of the position I am interested in. I like the company," he said, with a dashing smile. "Good night, Miss Christopher."

He lounged away at his athletic pace. Looking at his retreating form, Clara thought she had never seen such an exasperating gentleman. Or one with such a well-shaped head. Not round like an orange, or pointed like a pineapple, not flat-backed like a Teutonic head but a nice shaped head. She was gazing after him bemusedly when Maggie accosted her. She was already dressed in her pelisse.

"Has Ben been teasing you?" she asked.

"No, not at all. It is your turn for the inn tonight, Maggie. Don't let Nel cozen you she is hungry. She only wants to get downstairs for some reason. Early morning is the danger period. She slipped off on me around seven-thirty this morning."

"It's all right. Ben says Moore hasn't arrived yet."

Clara gave her a startled look. "Who is Moore?"

Marguerite put her fingers over her mouth. "Oops! I think I've let the cat out of the bag. I thought Ben would have told you about Moore."

"But who is he?"

"A handsome rogue," Maggie laughed. "And I wager you can figure out the rest."

It did not take Clara long to figure out that Moore was involved in some troublesome romance with Nel. She was not entirely sorry to be missing out on a sleepless night at the inn when she learned it.

Clara's chamber on that night was the dressing room next to Lady Allingcote's, vacated by Maggie. Lady Allingcote was already in bed with the adjoining door closed when Clara went up. Clara slept soundly and rose in the morning ready for another full day. She was not prepared for a new twist, however. Lady Allingcote made quite a point of sitting beside her at breakfast and engaging her in conversation. When Clara finished eating and rose to begin her chores, Lady Allingcote insisted on helping her make space for the wedding gifts in the blue parlor, where they were being displayed.

The lady was outstandingly friendly, and also markedly inquisitive. Clearly some indication had been made to her to get to know Miss Christopher. Clara could not but wonder at the reason for it; could not help thinking it was Ben who had put her up to it. It made her nervous, and she felt she was not appearing to best advantage. She answered the questions put to her briefly, but did not contribute much voluntarily. All her usual store of small talk dried up. She had thought she could converse pleasantly with anyone, but found that with Ben's mother eyeing her carefully, she had nothing to say. Her rootless life seemed suddenly shoddy. When the job was done, Lady Allingcote said, "When can you spare a few weeks to us at Braemore, Miss Christopher?"

Clara was dumbfounded at the idea. Lady Allingcote seemed to think her style of living was even worse than it was, that she would move in with just any chance acquaintance. Her being with Lady Lucker was already an imposition—only Oglethorpe's cousin. "I—I am to return to my aunt when she comes back from Greece, ma'am," she said.

"That's nice. I hope she will spare you to us for a visit. Maggie is very eager to have you. Indeed we all are, Benjie and myself, too."

It came to Clara's mind that Maggie always did as her brother asked. She had got on well with Maggie, but hardly so well that an invitation had been anticipated. "I really don't know. I shall have to wait till Auntie is back," she said, blushing pink as a rose. Her answer sounded ungracious to her own ears.

"It won't be too long, I hope. Sometime in January, if you can make it. I love to have company in January. It helps get through the dull winter. But we shan't be too dull. Benjie will show you around. He will like to do it." There was just some little significance in these last remarks, some inflection of voice

109

that implied Benjie was at the bottom of it all. It was enough to turn Clara completely mute.

Lady Allingcote smiled in contentment as she left the room. She was relieved to see Miss Christopher was a very nice young lady indeed. Not forthcoming, as she had feared, and while quite pretty, it was not a pair of eyes or a conning smile that had been the cause of her son's command to "Make Miss Christopher come to us." Odd Ben had never told her the lady's name before. He had mentioned, "The girl from the Bellinghams' " from time to time over the past months. Maggie used to tease him about her.

Lady Allingcote had been afraid she would find Ben's mysterious lady to be a slightly older, slightly sharper version of Nel Muldoon. She had come to dread the day she must meet her, but she had met her, liked her, and been assured by Charity that she was a lovely young girl with no airs or graces about her, before she even knew she was Ben's mysterious friend. Clara Christopher would do very well. Indeed if she had been found to do less well, no very strenuous objections would have been raised to a girl who might supplant Nel Muldoon in her son's affections.

Clara was happy to make her escape from this unwelcome bout of attention, but she required a little time to compose her thoughts. She went to her room, wondering if Ben had engineered the invitation and wondering whether she should accept it. She went downstairs half an hour later, eager for his return to Branelea, to see if he would add his own solicitations to his mother's. He had not returned, nor had

Maggie, who might have been subtly pressed for news.

Clara was soon caught up in other chores, and when luncheon was announced, the three from the inn came in, red-cheeked from a walk in the country. No snow had fallen yet, but the air was uncomfortably brisk. It seemed hard that the innocent Allingcotes should be so inconvenienced because of Miss Muldoon. Only Nel expressed any displeasure with her morning, however, and when Ormond complimented her on her good color, she too let on she had enjoyed the exercise.

In the afternoon, Clara was to go to the village for Lady Lucker. She decided that while she was about it, she would take her books back to the lending library. They were due that day, and no more than her hostess did she wish to disburse a penny when it might be avoided. When Nel heard of the outing, she pulled Clara off to a corner to hear a great secret. She would go with her, as she wanted to get Prissie a wedding gift. They had discussed it the evening before, which explained their five-minute talk without coming to blows.

"You have been out all morning. Why didn't you buy the present then?" Clara asked. She had hoped Allingcote might accompany her on the outing and was not happy to have Nel's company.

"We didn't walk in the village."

"Very well, but I'm leaving right away. You'd best get ready."

Clara sought out Allingcote to tell him the plan, hoping he would squash it. "Excellent," he said. "I was hoping someone would think of something to entertain her, for I am busy myself."

"I wonder if Herbert would like to come with us," Clara said casually.

"He has gone to call on relatives living nearby," he said with satisfaction. "Hearing there was a vicar in the house, Nel declined his invitation." She hadn't even the satisfaction of making him jealous. Herbert had asked Nel to go with him. "I am taking Mama to have Prissie's silver tray engraved," he continued, "and we must go to Woking to do it. Nel could come with us, but Mama particularly loathes her. She has managed to make herself unpopular in most quarters, poor girl."

"Including this quarter," Clara said grimly. There was no satisfaction in the meeting: no getting rid of Nel, no Allingcote to accompany them, no mention of the visit to Braemore, no flirtation at all.

His commiserating smile was the only ray of comfort. "You'll be careful?"

"Why, has Moore arrived?"

He looked at her sharply. "Who let it out, Nel or Maggie?"

"A little bird told me. You'd best give me his description, in case we run into him."

"If you see a brass-faced, black-haired, greasy hedgebird in high shirt points and nip-waisted jacket, driving an abominable spavin-backed pair of grays, that will be Moore."

"The village abounds in greasy hedgebirds. They are endemic to Brickworth. What is his build?"

"Tall and gangly, wearing a jacket with padding

112

to give him a set of shoulders. About twenty-five years of age. He leers a lot at all the ladies."

"He sounds appalling! What does she see in him?"

"To be fair, the less demanding girls seem to tolerate him pretty well, but then Nel has no taste."

"I don't know about that. She likes Herbert."

"Ormond is well enough, if you can stand his geniality." He changed his tack when he realized he was being irrational. "All the ladies like Ormond, do they not? You, Maggie, and I have even seen the nose twitchers in gray bombazine giving him the eye. But in Maggie's case it is his height that attracts her. She likes tall men, and like most statuesque ladies, is constantly pestered by ankle biters."

"I shall introduce her to my Major Standby. He is over six feet."

"Why not foster a friendship between her and Ormond? I have just told you she is thinking of falling in love with him. I think, that though you are too cautious to admit it, you have a secret passion for him yourself. His name keeps recurring in our conversations."

"She must wait till Nel is through with him. The line forms to the right. I shall keep Nel away as long as I can. I have to go to the library as well."

"You have a carriage? I mean Aunt Charity gives the use of hers?"

"Certainly. The hired help is not so badly treated as you think."

"Good luck," Allingcote said, and walked away.

Clara met Nel on her way to the hall, outfitted for the trip in a beautiful deep blue pelisse, lined in sable. What an elegant little creature she was and smiling today, too, in good humor with the world. Till she opened her mouth she was bewitching. It was praise of her generosity in giving Prissie a set of crystal salt cellars with silver-plated spoons that engaged her tongue during the trip to the village. She kept looking about her. Clara now suspected it was Moore she was looking for, and not just any stray admirer. As she did not officially know about Moore, she said nothing, but she kept an eye out for the man described by Allingcote as they entered the village.

Going to the village with Nel proved an experience Clara did not wish to repeat. Nel had to stop at every window to admire or disparage every item in it. She entered the shops to try on gloves, bonnets, and shawls she had no intention of buying. Ells of material were taken down from shelves and held up to her face to determine whether they suited her. Her beauty and flirtation created considerable stir among the male shoppers. She smiled at them all and turned around after they had passed to make sure they were looking back at her. She spoke in a loud, carrying voice, offering any comment that came to her about anyone, uncaring whether a passerby should hear herself called an old quiz or a dowd. She bought a ginger cake and ate it from her fingers, dropping fragments amidst the lace and ribbons, and in general made a vile nuisance of herself. She was finally dragged into the gift shop to buy the salt cellars, and from there they went on to return Clara's books.

At the library, an occurrence that provided some small pleasure took place. A gentleman of the first stare was perusing the stacks. As Nel did not immediately get a glimpse of him nor he of her, he began casting a few long eyes in Clara's direction. By judicious peeps over the top of a novel, Clara saw that he was ravishingly handsome. Tall and well-formed, with black hair sitting on a head nearly as pleasing as Allingcote's. He was elegantly outfitted in a coat of blue Bath cloth, wearing tan trousers, and carrying a coat over his arm.

No word passed between the two for several moments, but as they worked their respective way down the stacks, they both arrived at the novels of Scott at the same time. Clara thought it was perhaps not quite by accident that his hand went out right after hers to select *Guy Mannering*. She was charmed by this ingenious and respectable bid for acquaintance. He gave her a bashful look and said, "Sorry. You were first." His accent was obviously that of a gentleman.

"I have already read it," she smiled. "It is very good."

Despite his air of shyness, he was not slow to carry on and enlarge the opening. "Do you indeed recommend it, ma'am?" he asked, smiling to reveal perfect white teeth.

She recommended it very highly, though she had not actually liked it much. Scott soon led to Byron. Byron, of course, might lead to any mischief. Before long, he had led to an introduction. The gentleman was a Captain Carruthers, recently retired from the

Dragoons and about to set up housekeeping in the neighborhood. Clara had heard Lady Lucker mention some retired officer moving to the area. She volunteered that she herself was only a visitor and mentioned the wedding, as it occupied so large a part of her mind.

The wedding called to mind Nel Muldoon, and Clara thought it a good idea to get the chit out of the library before her eyes should fall on the handsome captain. There would be no getting her out without a pitched battle once that had happened. She excused herself and went to find Nel down among the gothic novels of Mrs. Radcliffe, right where she thought she would be. The captain followed Clara down the aisle at a discreet distance, and when Clara and Nel went to the desk, Nel spotted him. It seemed like fate that the two should stop and stare at each other a long moment.

Seldom must two such perfectly formed physical specimens come together. Nel's rosebud lips parted to show her teeth. A soft sigh of pleasure escaped, but she said nothing. The captain, waiting his turn at the desk, turned to Nel and smiled his charming, shy smile. Some few words passed between them. Clara was full of apprehension, but really nothing could happen in the two minutes she stood talking with the librarian. Nel was in full view the whole time, and all that was happening was that the captain was showing Nel his book, perhaps saying that her friend had recommended it. The captain looked in her direction at least. Nel seemed to be on her best behavior to impress him.

116

Clara took up her new books, bowed to Captain Carruthers, gathered up Nel, and left. "A very handsome gentleman," she said to Nel. "A pity he had not come into the neighborhood sooner and he might have ended up at Prissie's wedding."

"I never saw anyone so gorgeous!" Nel sighed. "Do you know him well, Miss Christopher?"

"No, I never met him before."

"He said he has lived here a month. What a slow top you are! I should have had him calling on me long since, if I were you. I wish I were staying a little longer at Branelea. I wonder if Ben . . ."

"I shouldn't think so," Clara said firmly.

They had been gone over two hours. By the time they reached home, it would be close to four. They went to the carriage and returned to Branelea.

Chapter Eleven

There was some little unpleasantness before dinner when Nel chose to present her wedding gift to Oglethorpe instead of the bride and did it during a moment when she found him alone in the blue parlor admiring his other new acquisitions. Prissie discovered them in the act of feeding each other imaginary spoonfuls of salt from the miniature spoons that accompanied the cellars. This activity was interrupted as soon as the bride arrived on the scene and snatched the spoon from his hand. She was only prevented from dashing the crystal cellar to the floor by her groom's presence of mind in pointing out to her that the gift was exactly what she had wanted.

The "Thank you so much" Prissie conferred on Miss Muldoon was chilly enough to cause goose bumps. With Oglethorpe reverted to his best behavior, Nel soon forsook them both and went in search of more amusing company.

Clara learned of the "little contretemps" from Lady Lucker, who had it from Prissie within minutes of its occurrence. Clara took upon herself the task of preventing further "little contretemps," before they should escalate to incidents requiring the services of a doctor. She watched Nel like a hawk. This was the very eve of the nuptials, and it was of the greatest importance that no rupture occur between the bridal couple at this late date. Nel required a deal of watching. She was even more mischievous than usual. Her blue eyes danced and an impish smile played over her lovely face. She looked half angel, half vixen, as she flirted outrageously with every man at the party. Herbert, Ben, Maximilian, and a dozen doddering old cousins were tickled pink with her ways.

Clara thought it best to get Nel off to the inn as soon after dinner as might be arranged. She met with opposition from Allingcote, whom she made sure would be a supporter in her plan. He had received, during her absence, a brief notice from the inn informing him that a certain gentleman had been making inquiries. The man had not registered, but he had been there asking questions, and Ben thought Branelea the best place for Nel.

It was when the gentlemen joined the ladies after dinner that Clara suggested to Ben they leave early. "Not tonight," he said. "Aunt Charity has a sort of party planned. Some of the neighbors are coming in. I shouldn't think you would like to miss it, Miss Christopher."

She had been looking forward to the party, but was on thorns with Nel's behavior and told Ben about the scene in the blue parlor. "I'll keep an eye on her," he said. "She will enjoy the party. There's no need

119

she must miss all the fun only because Prissie is spoiled, and Oglethorpe an ass."

"And herself a hoyden," Clara added curtly. It was obviously Nel he wished to have the pleasure of the party, not her. That the bride must be inconvenienced did not appear to bother him in the least.

"Nel is frisky tonight," he admitted, looking across the room at her. She had garnered Herbert Ormond to her side. "Did anything of interest occur this afternoon? You didn't see any sign of our greasy hedgebird?"

"No, nothing of the sort."

"No one tried to attract Nel's attention? She was not, perhaps, slipped a note or anything like that while your back was turned?"

"No. It was Miss Muldoon, who was trying desperately to attract all the attention herself, and my back was not turned. She enjoyed only one flirtation, not with a greasy hedgebird, but a very dashing captain. The whole passed under my very nose."

"A friend of yours? You know him personally?"

"I never saw him before today, worse luck. My visit might have been a good deal more agreeable had I made his acquaintance sooner. He is new to the area, a Captain Carruthers by name. I believe Lady Lucker knows him, or of him at least."

"Which of you was it who had the pleasure of a flirtation with him? You mentioned Nel, but your smiles intimate it was not only Nel."

"Very true. It will no doubt come as a surprise to you that I occasionally arouse a little interest from gentlemen myself. In fact, I met him first."

"Where did you pick him up?" No smile adorned his usually agreeable face.

"I picked him up—such a delightfully genteel expression—in the circulating library. One always feels that any acquaintance struck up in a library must be unexceptionable. I met some of my best friends there, over the tomes. Ecclesiastical gentlemen in the department of theology, scholars among the classics, and so on."

"Where did you meet Captain Carruthers? Was it in the romance department, amidst the marble-covered novels? Or would it be the history books that served as an introduction, down among the battles and wars."

"No, no. He is not at all gothic, or severely military either. More of a man about town. It was Sir Walter Scott and Lord Byron actually who introduced us. We smiled at each other over *Guy Mannering*, and got down to names over the *Corsair*—and a very apt place it was to meet, too. There was something of the corsair in my captain, except that he was a little shy. I have taken him on for my own, you see."

Allingcote became stiffer as the conversation proceeded. "What was he like?"

"Simply beautiful. Tall, broad-shouldered, handsome, marvelous smile, wearing—"

"Spare me the details."

"You *asked*!"

"I was merely confirming he was not the hedge-bird."

"There was not a speck of grease on him anywhere. I never saw a better-groomed gentleman."

"I didn't think he had been basted for frying. You didn't notice what the gentleman drove?"

"Alas no, but it ought to have been a white charger. We only saw him in the library. Nel was quite as infatuated with him as I. She said she never saw anyone so gorgeous."

"Then it cannot have been Moore. She would have let on to be disinterested if it had been him. She's obvious, but not utterly transparent."

"She is acting strangely tonight," Clara said, glancing across the room at her. "I hope Herbert keeps her busy."

"Don't worry. *I'll* keep her busy."

"Then I shall have my turn with Herbert. I promised him an hour of my time, and don't know when I shall have another free."

Ben cast a look of rebuke on her before walking off to Nel. He stayed with Nel for the better part of the evening, despite heavy competition from the neighboring bucks. Clara's small consolation was that Herbert appeared happy to be with her. She trusted Allingcote would not know that the dreamy smile on his face was due to Nel Muldoon, whose merits he extolled till Clara was ready to crown him. Over all, it was an exceedingly tiresome party, and with a late-night supper, it lasted well past midnight. Clara mixed among the other guests as a sort of assistant hostess, seeing that everyone had a full glass and that empty glasses were whisked out the door for washing. She had no helper that evening and felt ill-used at doing the same chores she had been doing for weeks with no reluctance at all.

She had many jobs lined up for the morning, and though the wedding was not to be performed till eleven o'clock, she was to be back at Branelea from the inn by eight-thirty or nine. One special duty that had somehow devolved on her was the mixing of the wedding punch. Three large bowls of fruit punch enlivened with wine and soda water were to be mixed up and served just before the wedding feast. The bride would be toasted in champagne at dinner, but before eating, the crowd would have a few glasses of punch to slake their thirst and lessen the quantity of champagne consumed. It was Lady Lucker's wish that the soda water be added just before serving so that the punch would effervesce. This, in some magical manner, was to remove the taint of thrift from the beverage.

Outside help had been hired (and borrowed) for the great day. Among their number was one man who professed to know something about brewing up a good punch. A chat with him had revealed to Lady Lucker that his punch was a heady brew comprised to a large extent of various wines. Her own mixture was to be mostly juices (not cheap either, she pointed out to Clara). Three dozen oranges and a dozen lemons, to say nothing of the pineapples she had had crushed. These had come from her neighbor's succession house, as had the oranges, but the lemons had cost hard cash.

With the aim of mixing the punch as the guests came in the front door, Clara was to sit well to the rear of the church and get herself into the first carriage leaving it. The removal of wraps and taking of

123

a seat in the gold saloon was all the time allowed Clara to mix her three bowls. The prospect of it unnerved her somewhat, as she had not before mixed punch for such a special occasion, and never in her life one of such strange ingredients. She knew the soda water to be the crucial item, and it was to be added last. She had received a dozen warnings not to let the professional punch maker take over on her and go adding extra wine behind her back. As the evening drew to a close, she went to the room where she was to oversee the punch making. She wanted to check that all was in order and that her apron was there. Splashes of juice on her rose gown would be the ruin of it.

It was late and Clara was tired. She was also unhappy with the evening just past and unnerved at the prospect of the morrow's busy activities. She saw her apron resting on a table and unfolded it to see it was a fresh one. Shaking it out, she examined it and refolded it with a weary sigh.

"Take heart. It will soon be over," a voice said from the doorway. Turning, she saw Allingcote had followed her from the gold saloon. He had been sparing of his attentions all evening, and she was surprised to see him.

"Not too soon to suit me," she said, replacing the apron on the table.

Allingcote advanced into the room and looked at the table, set with punch bowls turned upside down to keep out the dust, ladles, cups, serviettes, and all the apparatus required for the job.

"It takes a lot of work to put on a big wedding," he mentioned idly.

"Too much. If I ever marry, I'll elope."

His eyes widened in playful surprise. "This cannot be the cautious Miss Christopher contemplating such a wicked deed! You are overly tired."

"I am," she agreed. The thought flitted through her harried mind that if it were not for his bringing Nel here, she would be less fatigued. Or even if they had left when she suggested, she would have been tucked up in bed at the inn hours ago.

"An elopement is not at all the thing," he pointed out.

"I know that," she said curtly. "I was joking."

"Ah! It was your scowl that led me astray. Jokes are more usually accompanied by a smile, or at least an effort to conceal a smile."

"You would know, Allingcote."

Seeing that she was determined to be grumpy, he joined in her complaints. "I cannot imagine why Aunt Charity chose December for a wedding. And between Christmas and New Year's, too, such a busy season. Spring is much better, don't you think?"

From sheer perversity she answered, "No, I think this is a very good time for a wedding. Spring is a pleasant season, it needs no help, but the winter months are dull. A wedding enlivens things."

Allingcote appeared to be considering this remark with more weight than the speaker intended. "Yes, a little later in the winter, perhaps, after the excitement of the holiday season has worn off."

"No, no. Prissie chose an excellent time. There is

invariably a sense of letdown after Christmas, and a wedding, one assumes, would mitigate it somewhat for the married couple at least."

"You may be right," he said, frowning in concentration. "But it is a dreary season for a honeymoon. Where does one go in January?"

"In the case of Oglethorpe and Prissie, one goes to Scotland to visit relatives."

"Oh, the Highlands—they are miserable in any season. A pile of rocks and sheep and frigid winds, even in midsummer. In winter they are intolerable."

"Was there not some mention of your going there yourself? Your mother wrote you were going somewhere, I think. She was not sure you would be here for the wedding."

Allingcote directed a surprised and rather angry stare at her. "And you *still* didn't intend telling me you were here, knowing that!"

"Certainly not. Why should I tell you?"

"Clara Christopher, you should have your ears boxed. I have a good mind to do it," he exclaimed.

"How very civilized you have become," she said coolly, but something in her warmed at his angry outcry.

"A paper-thin veneer of civility, just barely covering the snarling primitive man beneath," he warned, but she could see he was no longer angry. "You know just how to puncture that veneer, too, don't you?" With a little laugh, he took her arm and locked it closely in his own to begin walking slowly toward the door.

The position in which he held her arm necessitated their walking so closely together that Clara's skirts brushed his trousers at every step. It lent an air of intimacy that embarrassed Clara. She wanted to disengage herself before they returned to the company, but her slight pullings went unheeded as he chattered on. "Prissie will be greatly disappointed in the Highlands. A pity one could not go to the Midi, but with Boney marching his soldiers back and forth and lugging his cannons about, it would not be conducive to romance."

"Nor even to safety. Napoleon is such a ramshackle creature he has purloined all the best countries: Italy, Spain, Portugal—he has a toe in them all, depriving winter honeymooners of a ray of sun. Really I don't know what option Cousin Oglethorpe has but to take her to Scotland."

"Did you like it? You spent some time there."

"It was not my favorite spot in the world."

"Where is your favorite spot in the whole world, Clara?"

That "Clara" sounded so natural on his lips that she scarcely noticed it. She felt she was in her favorite spot, locked to Ben's side, but when she replied, she said with all her usual calmness, "I like London as well as anywhere."

"I like London, too." He turned his head toward her and leaned down, as she had seen him do dozens of times, but the charm of it never diminished. "It's time to leave. Best get your things. Nel has gone for hers. I'll meet you here." He patted her hand and let her go.

What a strange man he was. But after ignoring

127

her all evening, he could still send her heart soaring with a few foolish comments about Prissie's honeymoon because she imagined they were discussing their own.

Chapter Twelve

It seemed impossible that Nel was not fagged to death after tramping in the fresh air for hours in the morning, shopping in the afternoon, and staying up partying till well past midnight, but she was still full of life. In fact, she was wide awake and almost feverishly active in the carriage during the trip to the inn. She chattered and laughed, peered through the window, and did not sit still or silent a moment. She reminded Clara of an infant who had had an overly wearing day and was using her last gasp of energy before sinking into sleep.

Clara had to be up early in the morning, and it occurred to her that she hadn't mentioned it to Allingcote. Presumably his driver could take her to Branelea and return later for himself and Nel. She suggested this, and he replied in an undertone that he wanted to speak to her privately before they all retired. It would not be easy to arrange, but perhaps at the door of her room she could manage a word without Nel's overhearing.

Allingcote went to the desk as soon as they entered

the inn. Clara and Nel went on upstairs. He was smiling when he left the desk, but before he was half-way up the stairs, some new doubt or fear came to nag him. The gentleman was not at the inn, but that did not mean he was not loitering about outside, with his spavin-backed team hitched up, ready for trouble. He tapped at Clara's door. She had managed to get away from Nel early. The girl was not in bed, but moving about in her room.

"I've been thinking about what you said," he told her. "I would like to take you to Branelea, but daren't risk leaving Nel alone here. It would be best if she slept till nearly time for the wedding. The less she's at Branelea the better. My driver will take you and return for us. A pity you won't have long to sleep, but this is the end of it. I shan't get a wink my-self, if it comes to that."

"She must be dead tired. Surely she'll sleep like a log tonight."

He shook his head ruefully. "No, she's too excited, and I should warn you of the reason for it. The pro-prietor just told me Moore has arrived. She may bolt tonight. I plan to sit up on a chair fully clothed the whole night long, with my ear to the door. I'll hear if she tries anything. You try to get some sleep."

"What, exactly is afoot between them? Is he an out-of-work actor, her future costar in the theater?"

"He is an out-of-work something, but not an actor, to my knowledge."

"So it is purely romance."

"A romance, far from pure on his side, I fear."

"And Covent Garden was a story to hoax me?"

"Not entirely. That was last month's scheme. This month's hopes are pinned on running away with Moore."

"What a shatter-brained girl she is!"

"She is," he smiled, tolerant still. "But she'll come around with time. She's not really a bad girl at heart. She'll settle down when she meets the right man."

"A pity Moore is not the right man," Clara said wearily.

"That villain! He's only after her fortune. A wretched, underhanded fellow. I'd gladly run him through."

This violent answer sounded very like jealousy. Really, it was hard to put any other construction on it. "Does she know he's here? Is that why she is on edge?"

"I don't know whether she knows or not. Very likely it was arranged between them that he would come. She expects him, I suppose. He's been inquiring here for her. The proprietor, on my instructions, denied having seen her, but the servants gave us away, so he knows she is here. He might try to contact her tonight. He mustn't be allowed near her."

Such jealous guardianship as this robbed the conversation at Branelea of any further charm for Clara. She nodded and closed her door. Nel came in a moment later to get her dress unbuttoned.

"What did Ben want?" she asked.

That a young lady who rifled through one's reticule also listened at doorways was no surprise. "He wanted some private conversation with me," Clara replied.

"I suppose he was telling you to keep a close watch on me," Nel said, smiling contentedly. "Ben is so jealous," she added, sliding a glance at Clara from under her long lashes. "We were supposed to be getting married, you know, Ben and I. It was all arranged, and then I met someone I liked better."

As Nel was being so informative, Clara did not bother with concealment. "Mr. Moore?" she said.

Nel pouted. "Oh, he told you about Georgie. I made sure he would hide it to protect my reputation. Yes, George Moore is the man. He is very handsome, Miss Christopher. I wager even you would admire him."

"I doubt that very much, from the description I have had of him," Clara replied, undoing the buttons as fast as she could. She wondered if Nel was telling the truth about marrying Allingcote. "Were you and Allingcote actually engaged?" she asked.

"Unofficially. It was arranged by his papa and my Uncle Anglin."

"His father has been dead for two years. What is the delay?"

"I was only fifteen at that time, so of course the marriage was not to take place at once. We were together a good deal later on. He loves me," she said, full of confidence. "You must have noticed how jealous he is of anyone I show the least partiality for. Your cousin Herbert, for instance. Ben hasn't a good word to say of him. But it is George he especially despises, because he knows I love him. Why, he has even taken the notion George is ugly, and he is really very handsome."

"You don't plan to marry Allingcote?"

"No, that is what has Ben in such a pelter, but he doesn't frighten me. I know how to handle him."

There seemed some element of truth in this proud boast. Allingcote was strangely reluctant to recognize Miss Muldoon for the bad-mannered hussy she was. His smiles for her were sweeter than they should be, considering her behavior. What but love could account for such blindness and for such anger toward Mr. Moore?

"I am very tired," Clara said, as soon as she had the buttons undone.

"A pity I—we didn't think to bring a little laudanum along, and you would have slept well."

"A great pity," Clara answered with a wary eye. It was a wonder she hadn't been drugged, but with the accumulated fatigue of the past week, she doubted she would stay awake long. She did stay awake long enough to hear Nel get into bed. She waited for the long, even breaths that denoted sleep, and heard only the squeaking of the mattress as Nel tossed and turned. The sounds continued for the better part of an hour. In vexation, Clara pulled the covers over her head, but still the noises from behind the curtain continued.

It had been approaching one o'clock when they got to their rooms. At two, the girl still hadn't settled down or allowed Clara to do so. At two-fifteen, Nel emitted a low moan. Clara pretended to ignore it, but it was soon followed by a louder one. If she were to get any sleep at all, she must see what was amiss and try to calm Miss Muldoon. No doubt she was hit with hunger pangs at two-fifteen in the morning.

Crawling out of her own bed, Clara shuffled into her slippers, pulled her housecoat about her, and went into the next room. "I feel sick," Nel said. Her voice in the darkness sounded weak.

"You had too much wine, very likely."

"I only had three glasses. I think I had some bad food. The seafood tasted strange."

Lady Lucker and Clara had been concerned about the food contributions piling up at Branelea. It was very difficult to ensure they were all kept cool. It was entirely possible that one of the dishes had become tainted. It occurred to Clara that food poisoning might be rampant at Branelea, a ghastly crown for Prissie's wedding. But her main concern was Nel, and she felt her face for any sign of fever. It was a little warm, no more. She was worried enough that she lit a lamp and examined the girl closely. There was a febrile glitter in her eyes. Upon touching her own forehead to Nel's, the difference in temperature seemed significant.

"You must get a doctor," Nel said weakly. She was doubled up now in real or imagined pain, clutching her stomach. "It is the seafood making me sick. I think it was poisoned."

Clara stood undecided. She felt it was a trick, a bid for attention—or worse, a chance to nip off. On the other hand, if Nel was truly ill, she must do something. While she stood undecided, there was a tap at the door and Ben stepped in. He was fully clothed, as he had said he would be.

"Nel says she's sick," Clara told him.

Another low moan came from the bed. Nel crawled

deeper under the blankets, covering her face with her arms. "Did you have a look at her?" he asked Clara calmly.

"Yes, she does feel a little warm."

Walking to the bed, Allingcote pulled Nel's arms from her face and placed a hand on her brow. "Stick out your tongue," he said. Nel complied, looking at him with her bright eyes as she did so, to read his reaction.

Like most laymen, Ben knew what the doctors did, but not why they did it. Her pink tongue told him nothing. "Where does it hurt?" he asked.

"Right here," she said, rubbing some indeterminate midpoint of her body, whose exact location was hidden by blankets.

"At least it's not measles," Clara said with relief. "I was afraid she had caught them from her abigail. It takes about two weeks for the symptoms to show."

A flash of interest gleamed in Nel's clear blue eyes. She remembered Tolkein's symptoms very well. After a moment, she began coughing into her fist.

"Too late, Nel," Allingcote said sardonically.

Clara frowned at him. "We thought it might be food poisoning from the seafood . . ."

"No, I think it is measles after all," Nel said. Her voice was a little stronger than before. She coughed again, with a sly look at her audience.

"What about the pains in your stomach?" Clara asked.

Nel slunk back down on the pillow and rubbed her eyes. "It's a little better. I believe it was the wine."

"Give them a good hard rub, Nel." Allingcote said.

"A pity you hadn't thought of Miss Tolkein's measles before you began your performance, and you could have had your cough going more convincingly and rubbed your eyes into the proper shade of red."

"She *is* a little warm," Clara reminded him.

"She's a humbug."

"I'm sick. Please call a doctor. Ben, go and get a doctor . . ."

The breathless voice was scarcely audible now.

"Maybe you should send for one," Clara said uncertainly. "There is no point taking chances."

"She's bamming us," Ben said with conviction. "After I have gone for the doctor, you are to be sent off for water or milk or some such thing, and she nips off on us. It is the same routine followed—"

Nel sat straight up. "You promised you wouldn't tell!" she howled. When she realized what she had done, she sank back on the pillows. "Oh, the pain is becoming intolerable," she moaned.

"You'll have a pain to match on your backside if you don't stop showing off and get to sleep!" Ben said angrily.

Clara looked uncertainly from one to the other. She would have appreciated some of this strictness from Ben earlier. To become a tyrant when Nel might actually be ill seemed wrongheaded. "Let us send for the doctor, just to be sure," she suggested.

"She is not sick, but she deserves to be, getting you up in the middle of the night like this."

"I wasn't sleeping," Clara said. She felt an urge to protect Nel, now that Ben was attacking her.

"How could you, with her thrashing around in

136

here, loud enough to wake the dead? I could hear her in the next room."

"I am so sick!" Nel shouted in a loud, firm voice. She sat straight up in her bed now, eyes flashing angrily.

"More sickening than sick, Nel," Ben said in a rising voice. "It's time to grow up and have a little consideration for others. You have put Miss Christopher out of her bed to come here and mind you, and she has a great deal of work to do tomorrow. Your stunt hasn't worked. We know Moore's here; we know you mean to go running after him like a common little baggage. Your trick hasn't worked, so you might as well go to sleep and let us do likewise."

"You're just jealous!" Nel taunted. "I won't marry you, so don't think it."

"You won't be asked, by me or anyone else of any sense if you keep on in this fashion."

"I *have* been asked."

"Yes, by Moore. What do you think is the attraction? Your big blue eyes? No, my girl, it's your big fat dowry. He'd marry a wall-eyed bedlamite if she had a full purse. If you had any sense, you'd have sent that caper merchant packing long ago."

"You're just jealous. All the girls like him. Maggie would have taken up with him fast enough if he had ever given her the time of day. But he only loves me."

"Maggie had the sense to see through him within two days. You are the only one simpleminded enough to fall for his threadbare tale. If he loved you, he would not ask you to run off with him. He'd speak to your uncle, like a gentleman."

"Thanks to you, Uncle Anglin won't see him."

"Thanks to you, Anglin is unable to see Moore or anyone else. And yes, I take credit for informing your uncle that Moore is a gazetted fortune hunter. Now lie down and go to sleep. I'm not calling any doctor. Miss Christopher is not going to leave you alone either, so you have no chance of giving us the slip tonight."

At this harsh treatment, Nel recovered entirely. She hopped right out of bed, wearing nothing but an attractive lawn nightie. With a shocked glance at Allingcote, Clara grabbed Nel's wrap from a chair and threw it over the girl's shoulders.

"You waste your time trying to introduce any semblance of propriety into the same room with Miss Muldoon, Clara," Allingcote said, staring at Nel with disgust.

"What do I care about propriety?" Nel challenged, lifting her nose at Clara. "I am not a poor relation who must watch her every step."

Ben took a step toward her, but stopped, as if afraid what he might do. "What do you care about anything but getting your own way? Running your poor old uncle into a heart attack, and pray save us the poor little orphan scene. It has ceased to impress me. Miss Christopher, having been an orphan herself since she was twelve, will not be conned with it either. You are a selfish hoyden. Your basic ill-nature has been strengthened by unwise people pandering to you, only because you have inherited more money than is good for you. No credit accrues to you because your father was wealthy. It is past time someone told you the truth about yourself, Nel. Your tricks were barely acceptable in a child. In a young lady, they are disgusting. *You* are disgusting to any person of any refinement. I have undertaken to get you to London to save your uncle further anguish. Once you are there, I wash my hands of you."

A tear trembled at the corner of Nel's eye, but her tirade soon told them it was a tear of anger at having her whim thwarted. "Don't think I care what *you* think of me, or her either." She tossed her curls briefly in Clara's direction. "Much I care for the good opinion of a penniless spinster who battens herself on all her relations. She didn't come to the inn to look after me either, but only to have an excuse to be with you. She has been tossing her cap at you ever since you got to Branelea. Everyone is laughing at her. I wouldn't be a bit surprised if she is sneaking off to your room after I go to sleep."

Allingcote lurched forward, then restrained himself with a visible effort. His jaw was rigid and his hands were clenched into fists. "Will you please slap this wench, Clara, before I do it myself."

Clara was too overcome to do anything physical. "I am rather careful what I touch," she said in a glacial voice. She stared in disbelief at Nel for a moment, till she had recovered sufficiently to turn on her heel and retreat to her own room. She could not help hearing what followed, however, for Allingcote's voice was raised very loud.

"That was unforgivable, Nel. You will go at once and apologize to Miss Christopher."

"I will not."

"Go!" His voice was muffled, but it roared like thunder.

Clara thought there might have been some corporal inducement as well, perhaps a shove or a tweak of the ear, as Nel let out a little shriek of protest. In a moment she came through the curtain, with Allingcote behind her, and apologized, not very convincingly.

"I'm sorry, Miss Christopher."

"That is quite all right, Miss Muldoon. One always considers the source of an insult before taking offense," Clara said in a scathing voice.

Nel appeared to consider this as forgiveness and returned to her room. Clara heard the outer door close. Silence reigned once again in the two rooms. For Clara, sleep was impossible after this scene of turmoil. It goaded her further to hear, in a short while, the peaceful, measured sounds of Nel's breaths. The impossible chit had fallen to sleep herself, after making sleep impossible for everyone else. She was not the least bit sick. Clara had no tolerance of hatred, but if she could hate anyone, it would be Nel Muldoon.

She lay awake for hours, thinking of the insults she had received. The sting was sharper for the tiny grain of truth in Nel's accusations. She had not exactly set her cap at Ben, but she had not discouraged his attentions as she should have. Even when she believed him involved with Nel, she had allowed him to flirt with her, to hold her hand. She had not come to the inn to sneak into his room, but the fact that he was nearby thrilled her. The awful possibility that Nel was right, and people were laughing at her was the hardest to take of all. So many of her friends and relatives assembled there, watching her make a fool of herself. On top of all the rest, a wayward lady would receive few invitations to visit. Herbert, the Oglethorpes, Maximilian—all had witnessed her behavior. Daylight had begun to filter through the curtains before she finally fell into a fitful, troubled doze.

At seven o'clock in the morning Clara awoke without being called. She got up into a cold room with no fire lit and no time to call a servant. She did no more than pat cold water on her gritty eyes and splash it on her hands and face before shivering into her gown. She ran a brush over her hair hastily, thinking to slip out unseen and make her wedding toilette at Branelea. She peeked through the curtains to see Nel sleeping peacefully, with her hands outside the coverlet, palms turned up like a baby. The dormant form had no charm for her now. She was tempted to empty the cold water jug on Nel, but restrained the impulse.

Noiselessly she slipped out of the room and down the hall. As she passed Allingcote's door, it opened. The face that looked out at her was as tired as her own. That wan face and his rumpled jacket said as clear as day that he hadn't slept all night. "Can I talk to you for a minute, Clara?" His voice was uncertain, as if fearing a rebuff. He held the door wide for her to enter.

"In the hallway, if you please. I would not want to lend credence to the rumor that I spend my nights trying to invade your room."

Ben stepped into the hallway. He looked at her and shook his head, with some weary exhaling of breath that was not quite a definable word. "What can I say? I'm very, very sorry, Clara. And after you have gone to so much trouble for her."

"You don't have to apologize for her. Her bad manners are not your fault."

"The whole mess is my fault. She is in my charge. I shouldn't have dragged you into it."

"Spilled milk," she said dismissingly. "I must go."

"I don't suppose you got any sleep at all?"

"A little. You don't look as though you did."

Ben just sighed. "My valet is coming a little later. I'll freshen up for the wedding and see if I can get my eyes wedged open with something. I'm taking her on to London tomorrow, thank God."

"Then we shall have the pleasure of her company at Branelea again this evening. At least Prissie and Oglethorpe will be gone. I expect I shall be in bed with a sick headache by then. I really must go now. I leave no message to be conveyed to your friend. Good-bye." She took a step, but Allingcote caught her arm and detained her.

"Clara," he said in a wheedling tone, "you can't let that spiteful girl spoil things for us. This is absurd."

Clara's eyes were heavy from lack of sleep, and her

temper was short. "I don't see that she's spoiled anything for you in any case, and I think my reputation will endure her scandalmongering. I would appreciate it if you could use your influence with her to keep her from repeating her stories, however. Now I really must leave."

"We'll talk later," he called softly as she hastened toward the stairway.

Chapter Thirteen

Lady Lucker rose promptly at seven on the great day. Like Clara, she dressed hastily to do a few necessary chores before making her grand toilette. She had a very nice ecru lace to be put on later, the material bought at a reduced price due to some discoloration of the bolt. By careful tailoring, the darker patch was completely hidden under her arms. With her orchid from a neighbor's conservatory and her pearls, the gown looked unexceptionable. Add her sable cape over the top for the trip to the church, and she knew that no words but words of praise would be said of it.

She had a cup of coffee and toast with Clara when Clara came down. They were the only two besides the servants who were up to appreciate this calm before the storm of activity. Lady Lucker had so many apprehensions regarding the weather, food, flowers, and carriages that she did not think to inquire for Miss Muldoon, and Clara was in no frame of mind to raise the girl's name.

"You'll see that someone takes Georgiana and

Gertrude up in their carriage to the church, Clara? The Allingcotes have two carriages for the three of them, and Maximilian is all alone. He'll find nothing but bone to pinch on that pair. Oh, and the punch! You have the receipt?"

"Indeed I have."

"The sparkling water goes in last, mind. I want the punch to sparkle. You must taste it to see it's sweet enough, but not too sweet. Oh and Clara, be sure you nip down to the kitchen when you have finished your coffee and see that Cook has breakfast started. Three kettles of water boiling and a good fire on. It is too early yet to start the gammon and eggs, but Maximilian will want a cup of tea in his room at nine. I don't see why guests must insist on having themselves served in their rooms at such a busy time. The pearls he gave Prissie are quite magnificent, however. He was always so fond of her. I had rather thought a small string of diamonds, but I have come to think a large rope of pearls is better."

Clara gulped her coffee and for the next couple of hours she hadn't a moment to think of anything but what errand she was supposed to be doing. She dashed about putting the final touch on flowers for the tables, checking the table settings, running to the kitchen to ensure the proper contributions were being served up, and sending servants upstairs later to see that everyone was up.

She saw Allingcote's coach drive up and made a point to be out of the way when Miss Muldoon came in. Nel was to share Maggie's room and abigail for the dressing. At ten o'clock, Clara went to Lady

Lucker's room, which she was to use for her own dressing. Lady Lucker had dressed earlier and Clara had it to herself. With no servant to assist her, she slipped into her old rose gown with the new lace, her pearls, and black patent slippers. She looked pale and drawn after her sleepless night. With a sense of daring, she dipped into her hostess's rouge pot. A rankling resentment lingered that she should look her worst for this special occasion. Bad enough she had to wear a gown two years old—would he remember it?—but worse that she looked haggard from lack of sleep.

She knew Sir James had been dressed and out of his room some time ago. He was pacing the gold saloon, trying to get everyone to drink wine. She decided to have a glass to brace herself for the coming activities.

At ten-thirty, she went down and ran into Allingcote at the bottom of the stairs. Freshly barbered and changed into his formal suit, he looked like any young lady's dream. He walked forward eagerly to meet her as she came down, as though he had been waiting for her. Clara felt a surge of pleasure when he smiled and reached for her hand. "Charming," he said, running his eyes over her. His close examination made her acutely aware of her appearance and highly dissatisfied with it. Was he looking at the rouge? "I was wondering what you meant to wear. This is exactly how I remember you from the Bellinghams'."

It was a perfectly innocent statement, even meant for a compliment, but to a young lady on the point of exhaustion, a reminder that she wore a gown two years old was not taken as high praise. "Your infallible memory fails you, my lord. Not *exactly* the same. The lace is new."

He was momentarily stymied, but being fairly quick-witted, he soon deduced her meaning. "I was not referring to the *gown*, Clara," he said, offended.

"Just another of your little gaucheries. They are becoming quite as noteworthy as your memory."

"Do you have a ride to church?" he asked, checking the hot retort that was on the tip of his tongue, for his own nerves were ragged.

"Yes, thank you. And in any case, I would not wish to share a carriage with your friend."

"Mama is taking Miss Muldoon."

"I am going with Maximilian," she said, and added to herself, "and will be black and blue by the time I get there."

"My carriage will be empty except for myself— and *I* don't pinch," he added, trying to lure her into a smile.

She refused to be cajoled. "As you are in a generous mood, perhaps you will be kind enough to take the other dregs of society with you, Miss Georgiana and Miss Gertrude."

"With pleasure," he said, still keeping his temper, but with increasing difficulty.

Clara swept past him with a nod of her head. Allingcote stood looking after her, an angry glint in his eyes. There was no time for Clara to have her wine. The carriages were being loaded and starting to leave by turns, as the passengers were called forth.

Maggie, wearing a bright expression, came prancing up to Clara. "Do tell me what happened last night," she said in an excited whisper.

"A little set-to with Miss Muldoon. She took ill, or so she would have us believe."

"Oh Clara, *she* told me that much! What *really* happened to get Benjie in such a pucker? He positively is not speaking to Nel, and she has been winding him round her thumb any time these two years. He would not be raving about 'unconscionable behavior' and 'whipping at cart tails' only for that, but he won't tell me what she did. Did she run off with Moore? Is that it?"

"No, certainly not. She didn't leave her room."

"She smuggled him in through the window then. That's what it is! Oh, the minx! Just wait till I tell Mama."

"No, you misunderstand. It was nothing like that, nothing to do with Moore—directly, I mean."

"Come now, Clara. Ben isn't in the boughs only because she let on she was sick. She's always shamming. What did she do?"

Reality was bad enough, but speculation was so much worse that Clara gave some indication of the truth.

Maggie's cheeks turned pink. "The trollop!" she said, furious. "I wish Ben had beaten her as he said he wanted to. Of course it would suit her down to the heels to have that scandal to spread about the countryside. It is really too bad of her, Clara, but frankly, if it has opened Ben's eyes to what she is like, it was worth it. No one would believe a word of her story anyway. You, of all people, are so cautious and well behaved. Well, it is obviously nonsense."

"I am happy to hear you say so, Maggie. Reputation is important to a lady in my—dependent position," she admitted, struggling for the proper word.

"No one would believe that faradiddle if the Archbishop of Canterbury himself said it, much less Nel Muldoon. Ben always doted on her in the most foolish way, only because she's as pretty as a little doll and he felt sorry for her being orphaned. Now he has come to see her in her true colors. I wish she'd run off with George Moore and have done with it. They are a good pair. Two monstrously handsome rogues."

"I understood Mr. Moore to be unattractive," Clara said.

"Unattractive?" Maggie asked, staring. "Oh my no, he is a very Adonis. As handsome as any Greek statue, and as devious as a Greek, too. Or are they the devious ones? Odysseus I have in mind. Devious anyway, but fatally handsome."

"Your brother said—but now I think of it, Nel *did* say he was handsome, only I was not sure I would agree with her taste."

"Well, Benjie dislikes him. Most men do, for some reason. Jealousy I suppose, the same as women always dislike Nel, even before they discover she's a shrew. Moore is tall, dark, handsome, with a divine smile—but it becomes less divine once you get to know him a little."

"Ben called him a greasy hedgebird," Clara said, confused at such conflicting descriptions.

"He calls him the hedgebird from his habit of lurking behind hedges, waiting for ladies to walk by. He also lurks behind potted plants at balls, and columns at church, and so on. Quite an accomplished lurker. I was in love with him myself one night. He's a good dancer, and nice and tall, too. Not one of those odious little ankle biters that tall ladies like me have to stoop down to. He told me I have eyes like brown velvet, but when Nel told me he had said she had eyes like blue satin, and Miss Holyoake eyes like green velvet, and we all three had incomparable skin like a damask rose, I began to find him less handsome, and a little shorter. I wonder if he used to be a draper—all that insistence that we are made of cloth."

"A dealer in fustian, obviously."

"With ambitions to handle silks and satins. Oh, there is Mama. I must go."

Clara prepared a smile for Lady Allingcote, but never delivered it. She was surprised to see Lady Allingcote was alone. "Where is Miss Muldoon?" she exclaimed. "Is she not going with you?"

"That was the arrangement, till she talked your cousin Ormond into taking her," Maggie said. "She always prefers to go out with a male when she can—and she usually can."

"We could not dissuade her, since we did not try," Lady Allingcote added roguishly.

Clara's racing heart settled down. Maximilian's carriage was next in the line, and with a tingle of apprehension for her escort's marauding ways, she went out on his arm. There was a Mr. Haskett, relative of Sir James, in the carriage with them. Clara took a seat beside him. Much as Max loved to feel feminine flesh between his fingers, he did not like to make a public spectacle of himself. She received no physical abuse till she was dismounting, when she felt a small wince, its strength diluted by layers of skirt and petticoat. She frowned at Max, and he winked merrily.

As she had to leave in the first carriage, Clara slipped into the backseat of the church. The guest seats were half filled, and she scanned them with interest, before turning her attention to the new arrivals. Her mind was a jumble. How would she talk herself into the first carriage leaving for Branelea? Supposing it were already full or the occupants unknown to her? It would have been better to make a definite arrangement. Herbert would have taken her back early—but she would not ask him today. She had no desire to be in the same vehicle as Nel Muldoon.

She should have accepted Allingcote's offer of a drive; she would not have minded explaining her job to him. This line of thought was so agreeable that she found herself going on to examine his every utterance since seven o'clock that morning—and highly satisfactory utterances they were, too. Her natural pique at being called a loose woman or worse should not be laid at his door. He had been nothing but charming from the first moment he had come up to her in the gold saloon three days ago and shanghaied her onto his desert island. Only three days ago! Impossible she had only known him for three days. Twice three days—she had known him for three days at the Bellinghams' as well.

He was very easy to get to know. Maggie was the same. She was already a friend, giving and inviting confidences. So unlike that sly Nel Muldoon and her George Moore. Strange what Maggie had said, "handsome as a Greek statue," and "a divine smile." As she mentally compared Ben's greasy hedgebird to Maggie's Greek statue, she concluded that Moore was probably one of those good-looking young men who lack any real elegance. He would have a flashing eye or a flirtatious smile to excite some interest from the fair sex.

Clara came to attention when Herbert Ormond was ushered down the aisle. On his arm was an elderly lady in peacock blue. There must have been four people in Herbert's carriage, Clara thought. Nel had found herself a new escort. She would be coming down the aisle any moment now.

Before Nel showed up, Allingcote came in, with Georgiana on one arm and Gertrude on the other, the two little gray mice. Clara's attention was easily distracted. She watched as Ben took his place on the bride's side of the church, with his mother and Maggie. He leaned over and spoke to his mother. Perhaps he didn't know Nel had arranged to go with Herbert. Clara was still watching when his head turned and he began scanning the pews behind him. She took the foolish idea he was looking for herself, but when he saw her, his eyes just hesitated a moment before moving on.

Soon he left his seat and walked back to the rear of the church. At her seat he stopped and sat down, frowning. "Where's Nel?" he asked. "Mama said she came with Ormond, but she is not sitting with him."

She might have known it would be Nel he was looking for. "Ormond just arrived. I expect she'll come down the aisle with whatever other gentleman shared the carriage."

Clara watched as Allingcote went to the rear door and peeked out. He was still frowning when he went forward to whisper something in Herbert's ear. She saw Herbert shake his head. On his face was a look of frowning incomprehension. Clara felt an awful turmoil building inside of her. Herbert knew nothing about bringing Nel! She had lied to Maggie and Lady Allingcote. She wasn't coming to the wedding at all. She was running away with George Moore.

Allingcote's frown was deeper as he came down the church aisle at a fast pace, heading for the door. Clara looked a question at him as he passed. He just looked and kept going. It required an extraordinary effort to hold her seat, but she did it. What was he going to do? More importantly, what had that wretched girl done? Panic rose like an angry tide. Nel was an unconscionable hoyden, but still—she was young. Clara had no wish to see her destroy her reputation, maybe her whole life. She told herself it was early to panic, and besides, Nel was not her responsibility. Carriages were still arriving. Nel might be in any one of them. Some difficulty with her toilette might have detained her. Ben would wait and bring her to her seat.

For five full minutes Clara sat on nettles, waiting expectantly and glancing frequently toward the door, while the incoming guests dwindled to a trickle. Nearly the entire congregation was looking toward the door now, with the hope of seeing the bride make her appearance. Oglethorpe was already at the front of the church, also looking over his shoulder. He looked very pale.

The organ swelled, and an excited babble passed over the gathered throng. Prissie, her face as white as her gown, began her trip down the aisle on Sir James's arm. Lady Lucker had intended to rouge her cheeks, but must have forgotten. Both bride and groom looked as though they had been leeched for the past month. The nuptial trappings looked fine though. Prissie's veil, bought at reduction for nine shillings, had been starched, garnished with fish-paste pearls from an old gown, and looked splendid. Maximilian's pearls were quite lovely. They were almost invisible against her gown, but would look well later with colors. One would never guess to look at Prissie's stylish gown that it had seen duty before. Countess Kiefer's wedding gown had been altered beyond recognition with a more stylish set of sleeves and a new sash.

Sir James had fortified himself for the ordeal by sufficient wine to make his cheeks glow, or perhaps it was pride that did it. While all these details were being taken in, there lurked at the back of Clara's mind the fact that Allingcote had not returned, and Nel had not shown up at all. Herbert, looking back, caught her eye and raised his brows in an unspoken question. Clara shrugged her confusion, he frowned and turned his attention to the bride and groom.

When at last the ceremony proper began, Clara paid only scant attention to it. Her eyes flew often to the door, and Herbert's went often to her. Just before the "I do's" were exchanged, Clara heard a click at the church door. Turning once again, she saw Allingcote enter alone. His face was white with dread or anger. He looked at Clara a long moment. She shook her head to indicate Nel had not come. He looked to the front of the church, his only glimpse of the wedding, just as the couple turned to leave. Ben slid into the backseat with Clara, to leave the aisle and church door free. "She's gone," he said in a quiet undertone.

The first words that occurred to Clara were "good riddance," but she was too discreet to utter them. She sat silent while the bridal couple went past, then went out into the throng, conscious of Allingcote's arm on her elbow, wondering what he would do now.

Chapter Fourteen

The churchyard was a scene of happy confusion. Everyone was rushing up to the bride and groom, congratulating them as they shivered in the brisk winter winds. Lady Lucker was struggling to get a wrap over Prissie's shoulders, for though the sun shone, that wind was piercing through her own sable. Sir James waved his arms at the wedding carriage, trying to work its way through the crowd to the couple. Clara and Ben took one last, long look over the group, in case they had missed seeing Nel in church. They soon realized she was not present.

Herbert Ormond strode up to Ben's side in a purposeful manner, and Clara listened while the two men discussed the situation in a brief, dispassionate fashion that sounded bizarre to her feminine ears. All the while she was conscious of the pressure of Ben's hand on her arm, as though he was afraid of losing her.

"You didn't find her?" Herbert asked.

"No, she's gone."

"What do we do?"

"Do you mean to help?" Ben asked.

"Certainly. Where do you think she'd go?"

"Either Gretna Green or London."

"She managed to meet Moore then?" Clara wondered when Ormond had been let in on the secret.

"She must have," Ben replied. "I took a nip to Branelea. They say she went off with a fellow in a carriage like his. The man didn't come to the door, so it must have been prearranged between them. I put my money on London."

"I'll check out the road to Scotland," Herbert said. "I'll ask Max to drive Mrs. Rattigan home."

"And the Snelley sisters," Ben said.

That was all. No bickering, no interesting details, no mention of other possibilities. Just facts and decisions.

"Good. We'll head to London. Come on, Clara." Already Ben was turning to walk away, while the bride and groom still stood in the center of the group.

"I can't go. I have to make the punch." Regret stabbed like a knife, to have to miss out on the chase. "Oh dear, I should have left ages ago."

"Go with him," Herbert urged. "A woman might come in handy."

"What about the punch?" Clara asked. Keen as she was to go, she knew her duty lay at Branelea, with the sparkling water and fruit juice.

"Let them drink champagne," Allingcote decreed, and pulled her away, protesting at every step, till at last at the carriage door he relented. "All right, go to Branelea. I shouldn't have asked you to come, but *be there* when I get back."

"Well—maybe I should go with you," she said, undecided. Nel Muldoon's future was surely more important than three bowls of punch, and if she could help . . .

Her decision was made for her. She was hauled into Ben's elegant carriage and was off down the road, without even passing her duty regarding the punch on to another. She knew it was abominable to serve Lady Lucker such a stunt, but in all her visits, she had never been in on a runaway match before, and it was so very exciting. And such a comfortable carriage, with velvet squabs, heated bricks, and a fur rug. She spent the next few moments mentally devising excuses to be made when she got back, then suddenly realized Ben was speaking and switched her attention to him.

"What beats me is how she got in touch with him. She can't have seen him. Ormond says she wasn't speaking to a single soul when she was with him. He was certainly not around when I was with her. He must have smuggled a note to her at Branelea, or the inn."

"Do you think she's run away to be married?"

"Certainly, it's not the first time."

"You never told me that!"

"I very nearly let it out at the inn. I promised Nel I wouldn't tell anyone. Even Mama and Maggie don't know. I only told Ormond."

"Why did you tell him?"

"He asked me. He wasn't taken in by our story of

her dashing away from school, once he realized she'd been out of school for over a year."

"I'm sure I asked you a dozen times what she had done!"

"It's different, Clara. He's a man. Now don't hit the roof. I had an inkling I would need his help, and as I hoped to get him to relieve me of her somewhat, I thought it best to take him into my confidence. If you had accidentally let something slip, every soul at the wedding would have known before the day was out. Nel would be ruined."

"I am not a gossip. I wouldn't have told anyone."

"You might have mentioned it to Maggie or Aunt Charity."

"Or inserted an advertisement in the papers for the world to read," she said, glaring.

"I was very glad I hadn't told you, with the agitated state you were in this morning. You must admit you would have done her an injury if you could, after her stunt last night."

"I am not so vengeful as that." Clara fell silent for a moment, but she was not considering her ill-treatment, as Ben thought. When she spoke, it was on a different matter entirely. "I was just thinking . . ." Ben's gray eyes lifted in interest. "This George Moore . . ."

"What about him? You said she didn't speak to anyone when she was out with you."

"She spoke to Captain Carruthers."

"Captain Carruthers ain't George Moore." He stopped speaking and stared. "Is he?"

"That possibility had just occurred to me."

"You said Aunt Charity knows him."

"She knows *of* him. She hasn't met him."

"I don't see how Moore could have latched on to his name."

"Your aunt didn't actually mention his name. She had heard of a retired officer coming to the neighborhood. That's all."

"From your description, the captain can't possibly be Moore."

"Maggie's description of Moore, and Nel's too, is dramatically different from yours. They both said he is devastatingly handsome, and so was Captain Carruthers. It seems an odd coincidence. Ben, do you think—"

A frown drew his eyebrows together. "Describe the captain to me."

"He was tall, about six feet, jet black hair, lovely blue eyes—the shade of bluebells, you know, not dark, but not light either." Ben's frown deepened. "Well dressed, very fine teeth."

"Oh God, it can't be him," he moaned, more in hope than conviction.

"He was not in the least greasy," she offered as encouragement.

"Clara, I didn't mean he greased his hair, or wore oil-soaked jackets. His manner is smooth, oily."

"His *manner*?" she asked, astounded. "Do you mean to sit there and tell me you described that Adonis to me as a greasy hedgebird?"

"If he's Adonis, I'm the King of France. He's a

demmed caper merchant, smiling and smirking and scraping his leg at all the girls."

"Captain Carruthers did not smirk. He had a very gentle, shy smile, and he was certainly a real gentleman. There was none of that self-conscious strutting of the parvenu trying to look at ease among his betters. About Moore, how are his teeth?"

"Just teeth—rather large, white, straight."

"I would not call the captain's teeth *large*. They were just the right size for his mouth," she said pensively.

"It's got to be him."

"It must be. Nel exchanged a few words with him. There is no other way she could have contacted Moore. At least I know who we're looking for. And as you have given me your description of his spavin-backed team, I shall be on the lookout for a bang-up pair of grays and a carriage of the first stare."

"The rig is dark blue," Ben said resignedly.

"Oh how could you give me such a poor description of the man? Have you no eyes in your head? Moore is the most handsome man I ever saw."

"You've made that amply clear, Clara," he snapped. "He's a demmed greasy hedgebird, and he's probably not Carruthers at all. God, how I rue the day I got saddled with that pest of a girl. I wish I had given her the thrashing of her life last night, as I wanted to. I should have broken both her legs. That would have slowed her down."

"How did you come to get saddled with her?" Clara asked calmly. She was becoming inured to his exaggerated speeches.

"Her guardian, Papa's good friend, is old, and not well since she was foisted on him. Seeing what a rare handful he had inherited, he invited me to his place, trying to convince me to take her on permanently, as my wife. She was fifteen at the time. It was just before I went to the Bellinghams', in fact. Papa was still alive then."

"What did you say?"

"I didn't say no at once, as I should have. At fifteen, she was less forward. She had a huge dowry, and she's damnably attractive, Clara. I don't understand why you ladies can't see it."

"I don't understand why you call Captain Moore a greasy hedgebird."

"Of course her manners were not polished then."

"Unlike the high gloss they now wear," Clara snipped.

"She was young, orphaned. I thought with time and effort, she might make a good wife. Till I went to the Bellinghams' and met *you*," he said. The last words, spoken in a tense voice, caused Clara to look up in surprise. She found Ben studying her with a penetrating gaze, and her heart raced.

"I had more or less indicated to Anglin that I would keep an eye on Nel," Ben continued, "though I told him immediately upon my return that I would not be marrying her. I hoped Mama would have her to Braemore for longish visits, and Maggie might become her friend, but she proved uncongenial company. They both took her in strong dislike."

"I can't imagine why!"

A muscular spasm moved his mouth. "To continue

162

with the saga, I visited Anglin and Nel as often as I could get away, took her around here and there when she came out of school last year, but there was never any question of marriage. Then Mr. Moore turned up from God knows where, but accompanied by an unsavory reputation. Duns followed him, you know, and soon a story of unpaid bills in the village. Nel was immediately infatuated, *having very bad taste*," he added with heavy emphasis.

"How did she meet him?"

"At a public assembly, initially. Anglin is now stricter about where he lets Nel go. Moore was allowed to call once or twice, before his reputation was known. Then he was denied access to the house. I don't know what Nel may have contrived about meeting him elsewhere. Two weeks ago, she vanished. Tolkein had come down with measles, you recall, and Nel was being looked after by one of the older servants. Nel said she was tired and wanted to lie down. She sent the woman to the kitchen to press some gowns. When they took food up to Nel later, she was gone. Anglin immediately sent word to me at Braemore. I dashed over and decided the best thing was to bolt my team to the border, for I was pretty sure Moore meant to marry her, to get his hands on her fortune. That is his line of business, attempting to make a runaway marriage with an unsuspecting heiress."

"I would not call Miss Muldoon unsuspecting now. Surely she realizes after that dash to Gretna Green—And why do you think they are not headed there again?"

"He's too sly to try the same destination twice. The biggest city offers the most places of concealment. I wager it's London. Poor Nel."

"Poor Moore," Clara retorted.

"She's still young, Clara. I know her being an orphan doesn't serve as an excuse with you. I expect I was more impressed with it than I should have been, but she is not calm and cautious like you."

"She's a featherheaded ninny."

"Exactly. If only Mama and Maggie—I wanted to help her somehow. Perhaps I felt guilty at not marrying her as Anglin wanted. Papa thought it an excellent match as well. She proved too much for Anglin. He had a stroke when she took off, and I was obliged to remain with them for the week before Christmas to watch her. It was during that time we got in touch with the Bertrams in London. They are related to her, a younger couple, which is all to the good. They agreed to take her on, but they were leaving town for the holiday, and so I had to bring her with me to the wedding."

"What happened when she ran off with Moore?"

"I overtook them at Brackley, just fifty miles away from Anglin's place. Moore's spavin-backed team made poor time. Of course it helped that Nel can never drive through a village without getting down to shop, and usually to eat as well. I tried to loosen a couple of his wonderful white teeth, but they're long-rooted. I managed to get her home before morning, and as it has been kept hushed up, she is not considered ruined."

Clara listened closely, and when he finished she

said, "I think you should have let her marry him. No, I don't though," she said reconsidering. "He's too good for her."

Ben's face was a mask of outrage. "Too *good!* Clara, he's only after her money."

"What of it? Lots of people marry for money, and he'd earn every penny of it. It is considered unexceptionable if a penniless beauty nabs a rich gentleman. Why should poor, beautiful men and rich ladies not be given the same privilege? I say Nel should be allowed to buy her penniless Adonis if she wants him. But I still think he's too good for her." As an afterthought she added, "I wish I could afford him myself, providing he is Captain Carruthers, of course."

"Upon my word, you've taken leave of your senses."

"Not at all. What is money for, if not to buy what you want? If Nel wants him and can afford him, let her have him. Don't try to tell me that *whatever* his character is, it is one shade blacker than hers."

"But she's a lady!"

"Is spending money the prerogative of men alone? This is news to me. I haven't much, but I spend it exactly as I wish, and would advise Miss Muldoon to do likewise."

"I always took you for such a sensible lady. You're as foolish as Nel."

"I have been a poor little orphan since I was a child," she said, assuming a sad countenance.

"You've become a brazen baggage since I last knew you."

"Only since I have had the advantage of Miss Muldoon's acquaintance. I see I have been much too nice in my demands on myself. But tell me, since you spent the week before Christmas with Nel, how did Moore get to her to arrange this second attempt?"

"It must have been on Christmas day. I could not take her to Braemore, for fear of disrupting the family Christmas. I made Prissie's wedding sound as enticing as I could, hoping to keep her from dashing off before I got back, and thought I had succeeded. Lord, what a time to be hobbled with her presence."

"You are in everyone's black books, except possibly Herbert's, by bringing her to the wedding."

"The wedding?" he asked, surprised. "I didn't mean that."

"What did you mean then?"

"I meant having her along when I finally found *you*, tumbleweed, after two long years."

"I have not been lost," she said in a failing voice, as some idea of his import washed over her joyful body.

"You have been lost to me. For twenty-four months I have been scouring this country and Scotland looking for you."

"I—I was only in Scotland for three months."

"I know it well. After Papa's death, and for the month before, of course, I had to be home tending to business. When I was free to begin looking for you, the Bellinghams directed me to Scotland. I went there in April, and very nearly fell into a totally different engagement, quite against my will."

"The Scottish squab?"

He gave a hopeful smile. "Have you been keeping track of me, too?"

"No, only listening to gossip. After I left Scotland, I went to Devon."

"As did I, too late again. I missed you by days, weeks, and months in Sussex, London, Devon, Scotland, Yorkshire. I never knew such a girl for traveling. Of course, I, unlike yourself, was not free to roam every day of the year. I had Braemore to see to, as well as Nel. I think you might have given me a clue where you were, Clara. You knew—you *must* have known at the Bellinghams'—how I felt about you." His voice was low, but his tone was ardent, and the glow in his eyes spoke of total sincerity. "And if not there, surely some of the messages I scattered about the countryside must have gotten back to you. The half of England knows I've been looking for you."

Her reply was breathless. "Short of sending you my itinerary, I don't see how I could have done so."

" 'The Maid of Lodi' might have served as an excuse. You could have sent me the words, as you *promised* you would do."

"What would you have thought of me if I had been so encroaching, writing to an eligible bachelor?"

"I would have thought you were pursuing the friendship a little, and would have been happy. Why do you think I expressed so much interest in the lyrics of a song? But writing to a bachelor would not be the cautious Clara's way, of course. You can't teach an old dog new tricks." This belittling metaphor slipped out unnoticed, till Clara gave him a look,

167

half-laughing, half-incensed. "Another of my left-handed compliments for you," he said sheepishly.

"Two in one. Old *and* a dog. You outdo yourself. It remains only for you to call me an ape leader, and I shall want for nothing more."

"Only if I may be your ape. Really I am not far from it. I feel positively savage to see you smile at Ormond, or call Moore handsome, or look at any other man. To tell the whole shameful truth, I was none too happy with Major Standby the other night. You must proceed with the greatest caution, Clara, or you'll have a homicidal maniac on your hands. I was always afraid that when eventually I found you, you would be engaged, or married or something. How does it come you are still single?"

Clara's emotions were in blissful turmoil at this declaration. The only possible cause for grief was that she might be dreaming. To conceal her overwrought state, she simulated annoyance and said, "Lord Allingcote, you have just asked the most despicable question in the world. Don't *ever* ask any lady over twenty that utterly gauche, hateful question, or you will see savagery that puts your little blusters to shame. I have received three very flattering offers, and I shall say no more."

"You don't have to say more. That leaves me free to imagine you have been waiting for me." He looked hopefully at her. "I said *imagine*, Clara, my dear. You must feel free to correct me if my modesty has placed me under a misapprehension."

"Of course I feel free," she replied, feigning obtuseness.

168

He scowled, but continued with his rant. "And what a long wait it has been! I lost track of you completely when your aunt married and went to Greece. I was beginning to fear you had become a stowaway, that the tumbleweed had taken to water, and I'd never see you again."

"You would not have followed me across water?" she asked accusingly.

"Even without a boat, if only I had known which body of water to plunge into. I nearly fell off my chair beneath the palm trees when you walked through that door into Auntie's gold saloon, Clara. I thought I had finally run mad and was seeing a mirage. Perhaps it was my oasis that put the idea in my head, but I had the strangest sensation you were going to dissipate before my very eyes when I got close to you. And after years of concocting romantic outpourings, what blithering inanity did I hear issue from my mouth but, 'Fancy meeting you here, Miss Christopher!' as though you were a mere acquaintance. I had a strong urge to throttle myself."

Her lips moved unsteadily. "You are possessed of these urges to violence too often, Allingcote. Fortunately you never carry them through. Nel, Moore, me, yourself—the world would be sadly decimated if you committed half the acts you threaten."

"It's that savage I told you of, lurking beneath my well-cut jacket. A wrong word or look and I revert to the jungle beast."

She patted his hand in a maternal fashion. "But a harmless little beastie."

"A tiger on a leash," he countered. "Don't push me

too far. I very nearly locked horns with Ormond when he was urging you to go out with him and write him letters. I didn't want you to suspect I was a callow youth and tried to let on I liked him. I did, actually, when he verified your claim to be no more than friends. But you distract me from my story."

She gave a sigh of well-simulated impatience. "I thought we had had the whole story by now."

"No, no. We are just coming to the best part—the climax! The hero and heroine meet in the middle of a crowded room after years of involuntary separation. Involuntary on my part at least. We hear bells ringing, heavenly hosts of angels singing, the scent of roses on the air."

"And my hero says, 'Fancy meeting you here, old girl. Care for a glass of sherry?' "

"That is what I said, but I wanted to bolt you to my side with chains of forged steel."

"How convenient."

"With Nel on the other side, it would have proved an awkward arrangement. I had to be pushed out the door with her and told—not very politely either, considering the silver tea set *and* the Wedgwood cups—not to show my nose a minute more than was necessary."

"The Wedgwood cups? Countess Kiefer gave her the cups."

"So did I. Don't interrupt. In any odd minute I did fight my way in, Aunt Charity had you hopping. I had hoped you would not take Nel in aversion, that you might accompany us on a few outings. You would have liked the Roman Museum, I think."

"Think again. I didn't care for it in the least when Sir James made me go with him—three times."

Allingcote frowned heavily. "Don't be difficult, woman. I'm trying to make love to you. You would have liked it with *me* for a guide. We need not have gone inside and looked at the bric-a-brac. Museums are best appreciated from the window of a carriage. But of course Nel managed to get your hackles up, too. When both you and Maggie tore off on me the minute I came into the room that first evening after dinner, I knew my plan was futile. What had she said, by the way?"

"A great deal about the many accomplishments and gowns of Miss Muldoon."

He shook his head. "Her little scene last night didn't help, but I don't think it fair that you took it out on *me*. You were not at all kind this morning, Clara, only because I inadvertently mentioned your gown was two years old. It has held up remarkably well, incidentally," he said, fingering a fold in her skirt while laughter lurked in the depths of his eyes.

"It has seen a good deal of wear, too."

"You want to tell Aunt Charity where you buy such durable goods. But it was your face I meant looked the same, and your hair. You wore it like that at the Bellinghams'."

"Then the style is two years old. How time flies. I shall have it rearranged next quarter allowance."

"You don't have to change it to please me."

"I think Captain Carruthers preferred Nel's tousled locks. I shall try the Méduse do."

"You will have your ears boxed into cauliflowers

171

to go with it if that man's name crosses your lips again this day. This little veneer of civilization is thin and corrodes at a touch. *Jealousy*, Clara, is the corrosive agent, in case you have failed to notice it. Now enough sweet talk. What place is this we're coming to? Chertsey. No, we haven't been traveling long enough to overtake them yet."

"If his team is half as good as I think from your way of describing it, they will be three-quarters of the way to London. I wonder when they left."

"Nel would have waited till most of us were gone, to lessen the chance of being caught. She couldn't have left much before eleven. It's twelve-thirty now—an hour and a half. With that broken-down pair of hacks he drives, they wouldn't be farther than twelve miles at the outside, and that's springing them. We'll catch them up at the next village."

"If they didn't head for Gretna Green, that is," Clara said.

"London's closer. He'd head for London."

"They've outwitted you on every point so far. Let us hope you're right this time."

Ben gave her an accusing look. "I sense a little lack of trust here, Clara. A lady in training to be a wife has to suspend her common sense a little. Just because I'm a fool, there is no need to show your disrespect."

"How wives can put up with it, I'm sure *I* don't know," Clara said, and looked calmly out the window while Allingcote composed more mental violence.

Chapter Fifteen

East Chertsey was only five miles farther along the road. With no snow or other adverse conditions to slow their progress, they were there in not much above thirty minutes. The driver stopped and Ben sent him into the inn. "I don't expect they will be at the inn, but we'll stable the team there and tour the shops. Nel is an inveterate shopper."

"Surely Moore would not let her go shopping in the middle of an elopement," Clara objected.

"I thought you were coming to know Nel. She bought a bonnet on her last elopement. A very fetching one."

Clara chose not to hear this. "If it is really a runaway match, it is Herbert who will catch them. How could Moore think to marry her in London? She's under age, and Anglin wouldn't give his consent."

"He might be forced to, if they spend a couple of nights together before we find them," he answered in a hard voice.

"Is he really as bad as that?"

"Are you becoming disenchanted with Adonis?

173

That is how these fellows work. And Nel is not quite so wicked a girl as you think. She has no idea what that would do to her reputation."

"Every young lady is warned of the danger of remaining away overnight without benefit of chaperon."

"He'll have told her some cock-and-bull story about taking her to a respectable home. They were supposed to be stopping off with assorted relatives conveniently scattered along the route to Gretna Green the last time. She was too naive to suspect anything. I caught them around midnight—not with any relative. Nel's an idiot. I don't know how you got so wise, Clara, but I do think Nel's having no mother has made her not so well-informed as she might otherwise be."

"There are none so deaf as those who will not hear," she retorted. They vainly scanned the street up and down for a dark blue carriage and gray team. Finding none, they ducked quickly into the shops. There was no word of the elopers having been in.

Allingcote's groom came running down the street, with an excited air. "Are they at the inn?" Clara asked.

"No, ma'am, but his carriage is stabled there."

"They must be out eating then. Get the rig set to leave," Allingcote ordered.

"Lucky them," Clara said weakly. She was becoming increasingly aware of a large hole where her lunch should have been. She pointed out an elegant restaurant on a corner. Allingcote's eyes meanwhile had traveled across the street to a less genteel establishment. A hand-drawn sign in the fly-spotted window said, "Meals and Ale, Cheap."

"He wouldn't have taken her there," she exclaimed.

"Would he not? Moore's pockets are to let, and as I talked Nel into spending most of her blunt on Prissie's gift, I hope she cannot finance him."

"The one generous act I have been giving her credit for is buying that gift."

"To do her justice, she didn't put up much of a fight. Of course, she had no idea why I suggested it."

"She couldn't have been shopping this morning then, could she?"

"She could talk a shopkeeper into giving her credit, but she doesn't really care much what she buys. A twopenny ribbon or button satisfies her as well as a gown. This might be unpleasant," he warned, as they hastened toward the door. "Would you prefer to remain outside?"

"Certainly not! If any of the captain's teeth are knocked out, I shall pick them up for a keepsake. Perhaps I can be of some help in hitting Nel as well."

"Keep a sharp eye on her and make sure she doesn't slip out the back door or she'll steal a rig and escape us."

A steamy aroma of cabbage and grease assailed them when Ben opened the door. It was accompanied by a cacophony of rude voices and rude speeches. The place was crowded with lunch takers, and larger inside than it looked from the exterior. It was a long, narrow place. Grimy sawdust formed a carpet on the planked floor. The tables were of plain deal, on which every cup and fork made a clattering noise. A cursory examination of the front tables revealed workmen in fustian jackets. Ben and Clara walked slowly toward the rear, looking to left and right as they went. Before they were halfway down the room, Nel rose and waved to them, smiling brightly. Her pretty plumed bonnet and pale face stood out like a pearl in a bunch of agates.

"Here we are," she called. "Are you looking for me, Benjie? I'm so glad you came. The stupidest thing! George has no money to pay for our food, and I haven't got enough. I bought the sweetest little fan in a shop, which I wouldn't have done had I known George was short. It was no good anyway. It's broken already."

"Come outside," Ben said, grabbing Nel's sleeve, but directing his speech to Moore, who was none other than Captain Carruthers, looking as handsome as ever, if somewhat stunned.

He rose with a placating smile. "My lord, an unexpected pleasure," he began, in a very civil way.

"We'll continue the pleasure outside, if you please."

Moore turned his dark eyes on Clara. "I believe we have met previously, ma'am," he began. Clara could only stare to see him attempt to make a social occasion of being caught in a runaway marriage. She couldn't find a word to say, with Ben's knowing eyes just flickering a quick laugh at her poor judgment.

"You remember him, Miss Christopher?" Nel laughed.

"Come along," Ben said impatiently.

"We are faced with a rather embarrassing predicament," Moore offered sheepishly. Already his smile appeared less divine to Clara. It had the ingratiating, almost cringing air of the supplicant. She disliked to see such a fine male specimen sunk so low.

"No, Moore, *you* are faced with an embarrassing predicament," Ben countered. "*I* am faced with the rapture of rearranging your smiling face. Get your wrap," he said to Nel.

She handed it to Clara to hold for her, while she looked on in amusement at the scene going forth at the table. "Would you like to see my fan?" she asked Clara.

"No, I wouldn't."

The other clients were already showing interest in Moore's table, and Clara wished they could all go outside at once. Moore, apparently fearing too much privacy, retained his seat. "I am not leaving," he said, and picking up his fork, he began to eat his stew. Only the unnaturally rosy hue of his cheeks betrayed his discomposure.

"Leave him," Clara urged Allingcote. The shocked look he gave her indicated this was far from being his intention. "We don't want a scene. Let us get back to the wedding. You cannot beat him up here."

"Yes, I can."

"I'm going back with them, George," Nel said nonchalantly. "It won't be any fun getting married with no money. I have decided I want a nice white gown like Prissie's, and lots of guests. You know I said I would not go to Gretna Green again, and I don't want to stay with a vicar and his wife in London for a week either. It sounds very boring." She turned to Ben. "We were going to stay with George's uncle, Reverend Collier, till George could raise the recruits. It means get money," she explained to Clara. "George thought he could raise quite a bit of wind with my pearls and watch, enough to get married."

Nel's story inflamed Allingcote anew. "Are you stepping outside or not?" he asked Moore, in a truculent way.

Moore, feeling himself safe, smiled superciliously. "I am afraid not, my lord."

Nel turned a scathing eye on Moore. "George, you are surely not afraid of Allingcote!" she exclaimed in a loud, derisive voice.

"Let us go," Clara begged in a lower tone. Glancing at Nel, she saw the mischievous light in her eyes and knew the girl was preparing a scene of high melodrama. Her heart sank to her shoes.

"Take a good look at your Adonis, ladies," Ben grinned, but the only lady he regarded was Clara. In his eyes she saw mirrored Nel's mischievous expression. "Here is your Prince Charming." Her hopes for escaping the restaurant without a scene were not high, and though she despised Moore, she could not quite rid herself of a trace of pity for him. "I think Prince Charming wants a crown, don't you?" Ben asked her. He turned to examine Nel's plate with a truly wicked grin.

"Ben, don't!" Clara said, and put a restraining hand on his arm. A good part of her life had been devoted to avoiding such scenes as she saw developing before her.

"Do!" Nel squealed, having also discerned Ben's intention.

Ben stood undecided, looking from Nel to Clara, as mercy warred with a desire for revenge. Every fiber of his being wanted to land that plate of stew on Moore's handsome head.

"Don't!" Clara said, with a tightening of her fingers on his arm. Reluctantly he turned from Moore with no more than a look of disgust.

Left unobserved for an instant, Nel picked up the plate and dumped meat, gravy and potatoes, onions and carrots over Moore's head.

"That will teach you to call me a flat," she declared melodramatically, while peeping around the room to see that her act was appreciated, as indeed it was. The rough crowd even gave her a round of applause. She made a playful curtsy, took Allingcote's arm, and without a backward glance at her erstwhile lover, she paraded in triumph from the room.

As Clara was already hanging on Ben's other arm, she, too, was pulled from the scene. Over her shoulder she cast one last, commiserating glance at Moore. He sat as still as a statue. Only the stew moved, dripping in lumpy blobs from his nose and chin, and mercifully concealing his face.

"I don't like him above half," Nel told them in her trumpeting voice as they all hastened toward the doorway. "He scolded me for spending my money on Prissie's wedding gift, as though it were *my* place to provide funds for our elopement. He would not pawn his watch either, but only wanted to hawk mine. I was never so taken in in my whole life. I don't think he *loved* me Ben," she said, a tear welling up in her beautiful blue eyes.

Ben held the door and they all left. "I wonder why that would be?" he sneered.

As tears elicited no sympathy, Nel laughed instead. "He hasn't a penny to pay for that lunch, and his jacket is a mess, too. I wonder what he'll do."

They walked briskly along the street. "Make up to some other lady before he leaves, I expect, and feed her a Banbury tale. I wish you had let me knock him down at least, Clara."

"I don't see why Captain—Mr. Moore should take all the blame, or all the suffering," she replied.

"All the suffering!" Nel gasped. "I have been in agony fearing you would not come in time to pay the bill. George said we would have to wash the dishes if I didn't give him my pearls to place on the oak. It means to hawk. These pearls were a gift from my dear mama," she added in a hushed voice, looking for sympathy.

"Perhaps Moore's watch was a gift from his dear papa," Clara suggested.

Nel gave a hard laugh. "More likely he stole it."

Their carriage was waiting at the driveway of the inn, and they all got inside to return to Branelea. "We'll miss the wedding feast," Nel said. "I should have finished my dinner before leaving. The stew was not half-bad. I'm starved. Ben, could we stop at this place across the road? It looks much more elegant than that horrid place George took me to."

"No," Ben said baldly.

"Just for coffee . . ."

"We'll be home within an hour. You're not hungry, Clara?"

She was, but was more eager to get home than to eat, and let on she was not. The return trip was enlivened by alternate bouts of pouting and merry chatter from Nel, and by Allingcote's repeating that there was nothing to laugh at. That Nel had spoiled Prissie's wedding was a great joke to her, and that Herbert Ormond was even now out scouting the road to Scotland a marvelous thrill. She finally fell silent, fabricating a tale of kidnapping to entertain Mr. Ormond, and make him love her madly. As they passed the church where Prissie had been married, Nel mentioned this story to her rescuers.

Ben gave her a repressing look and said, "You have been ill. And if you don't want to end up in a convent, you'll tell the same lie as the rest of us. You had a relapse of whatever ailed you last night. Clara has been looking after you as your abigail is not with you."

"I notice it is Clara and Ben now, between you two. Congratulations, Clara. I'm sure I hope you'll both be very happy," she said. Her tone implied the virtual impossibility of anything of the sort.

Clara ignored her and said to Ben, "What is your excuse for not gracing the head of the second table?"

"Help me. Where have Ormond and I been?"

"Going for a doctor for me," Nel suggested, naturally thinking of a story that featured herself as heroine.

"For three hours?" Clara asked.

Nel saw that her helpers were sadly lacking in

181

imagination and gave them a hand. "They went to London to fetch Doctor Knighton. He serves the Prince Regent, you know. Perhaps I have a very rare disease . . ." Her eyes half closed and her face sagged into a good likeness of a consumptive.

"It had best not be contagious," Clara mentioned.

"Egomania, I believe it's called," Ben said.

"The unknown illnesses are the most romantic," Clara continued. "Some mysterious ailment that causes—"

"Inexplicably freakish behavior," Ben supplied.

"I was going to say faintness, dizzy spells, agonizing pain," Clara added.

"Yes, yes, that's it!" Nel urged. "Pains of excruciating agony. But by six or so I must feel much better. These attacks come and go with no regularity. I mean to be downstairs to see Mr. Ormond this evening. Must he know the whole truth, Ben?"

"He does know it."

She was quiet a moment, then said, "It was all George Moore's fault. He is older, you know. He took advantage of my youth and innocence."

"How did he get in touch with you?" Ben asked.

"Oh I am so very clever," she crowed, forgetful of her innocence. "He knew I was coming to the wedding and hung about the village waiting for a chance to speak. When I spotted him, I pointed in the most surreptitious way to the books Clara was carrying. George, who is also very clever, knew right off I meant we would go to the library. He went on ahead and waited for us. I was afraid you wouldn't speak to him, Clara. I nearly died laughing to see him wind you around his thumb."

Allingcote gave Clara a frowning look, and Nel continued. "When you were busy at the desk, I told George I would escape that night from the inn and meet him in the stable, but in case I could not get away, I would leave him a note. So when you wouldn't believe that I was ill, I just went to sleep and left a note and a shilling under my pillow next morning before we went to Branelea. I whispered to a servant girl on the way out to give the note to Moore and the shilling was hers. She already knew there was something odd about us. I told the stupid wench you two were holding me by force, and she believed it. You were my wicked stepmother, Miss Christopher."

"Who was I?" Ben asked.

"You were trying to force me to marry you, of course. And George was my rescuer."

"You got the characters mixed, but the story is not too far from the truth," Ben commented.

"Well, George wasn't forcing me, Ben." Then, recalling her innocence and youth, Nel added, "Not exactly forcing that is to say, though he was very insistent."

"I hope it's been a lesson to you," Ben said. "You may be sure there was no Reverend Collier in London."

"There must have been. He had no money for a hotel."

"There was your mama's pearl necklace."

"I don't know how you could be such a simpleton,"

Clara remarked, in her usual calm manner. "Any gentleman who tries to get you to elope with him, Miss Muldoon, is up to no good. I would bear it in mind in future if I were you."

"Bear in mind as well, Clara," Ben added, "that an acquaintance picked up in a library is not necessarily unexceptionable."

As the carriage rolled up the drive of Branelea, Ben said, "We'll all go to the stable and sneak into the house the back way."

They followed this plan and entered the house without causing wonder to anyone but the servants, and they were too busy to do more than look.

Chapter Sixteen

Dinner was over by the time the three refreshed their toilettes and went belowstairs. Clara's first concern was to discover Lady Lucker and tender humble apologies for her defection at the punch table.

"Maggie and I figured out what must have happened," Lady Lucker replied. "It was fortunate I got back in time myself to oversee the mixing of it. It was a great success. Between Georgiana and Gertrude, they have drunk up nearly the whole of it, but at least it kept them out of the good wine." The affair was proceeding so well that she had no more serious complaint than this.

"I see the saucy baggage is back," she continued. "It would serve her well to be stuck with a runaway match. We have been putting about that she is ill, and you were upstairs with her. Everyone has been asking for you, Clara. Just like Nel Muldoon to come landing in in fine fettle, but I did not actually say what was wrong with her, so we can say it was bad food, or something that passes quickly. Make sure you say the bad food was taken at the inn, not here. Where did you catch her?"

Clara told the story, omitting only the stew over Mr. Moore's head, not to spare Nel, but to spare the gentleman.

Lady Lucker nodded. "Maggie suspected it was so when the three of you vanished, and suggested the illness story. But do tell me, have you any notion what happened to Mr. Ormond? He is gone, too? Four great gaping holes at the table, but none of them at the head table, fortunately. I don't believe it caused much talk."

"He went north looking for Nel. Is he not back yet?"

"No, the gudgeon is probably halfway to Gretna Green, but I shall keep an eye peeled for him and tell him what we are saying if he comes. You must be starved, Clara. I'll have cook take you a bite into the morning parlor. I daresay Ben and Miss Muldoon will want something, too."

Ben, when apprised of the plan, certainly did, but Nel was too happy describing her mysterious illness to succumb to mere starvation. She had collected a large circle of sympathizers, comprised of every eligible male at the party and a few ineligible ones as well. Maximilian put an arm around her shoulder and told her he knew what would cure her: a glass of champagne, that was the thing. She also got a good sharp pinch and called him summarily to account for it in a loud voice.

Max thought it a marvelous joke to be called an old libertine and said if he were forty years younger,

186

by gad, he'd show the young fellows the way. "You are a pretty little kitten, miss. A bit thin, but not flat-chested in the least. A woman without a bosom is like a bed without a pillow. Nowhere to lay your head."

In the morning parlor, Ben said, "I managed to get a seat beside you after all. Major Standby will have his nose out of joint. Do you want some of this jellied salad?"

"Yes, I must try Mrs. Hinton's famous jellied crab."

"Who is Mrs. Hinton?"

"The lady who contributed the jellied crab. That is all I know of her. And I'll have some of the Nesbitt's Westphalian ham, too, if you please. I could eat a horse."

He placed a slice of ham on her plate. "Did no one think to contribute some Tewksbury mustard to the party?" he asked, looking around the table.

"We are using our own mustard. Would you like some of these prawns? Lady Gloria's cook is said to have a special way with them."

He tried one, but found nothing special in it, unless it was its coming to the party without expense. "Here, have one of Mrs. Smith's buns, and some of Mrs. Jones's butter," he went on, passing along every item he could reach. "I see a wedding feast is not the expensive affair I feared. There is almost enough left over here to toss another small do, don't you think?"

"Almost, but Prissie is the last girl to go, and when

Charles takes a wife, it will be his bride's mama who has to supply dinner."

He directed a meaningful smile at Clara. "Only if his bride has a mama." She was allowed by the job of eating to disregard any significance in this leading remark.

While they were still at the table, Mr. Ormond came in. "Lady Lucker told me you were here. I am vastly relieved to see you have got that poor child back safe. I met with no word of Moore's carriage and turned back before I got to Maidenhead. I trust you gave Moore a taste of the home-brewed, Allingcote?"

"Speak to Clara. She forbade it."

"Clara!" Ormond turned a shocked face to her. "This is not like you, to countenance such wanton behavior. The wretched creature must be made to pay the price for his villainy."

"He has paid for it," she said coolly.

"If he still draws breath, he has not paid in full," Ormond declared, high on his dignity.

"You're ranting like the hero in a bad melodrama, Herbert," she said dampingly. "Mr. Moore was left in such circumstances that any further punishment would constitute cruelty. Nel dumped her dinner over his head in a public restaurant. Sit down. We are putting our dinner to better use. You must be hungry, too."

"Good for Miss Muldoon! I never saw such a spirited girl. She is as merry as may be, showing no signs of the dreadful ordeal she has been through," Herbert continued, taking a seat.

"She was not kidnapped, you know," Clara pointed out. "A couple of hours in the company of the man she planned to marry until a few hours ago is not likely to induce a bout of melancholia. I think it is Mr. Moore who must be pitied."

"Pitied!" Ormond howled. "The man is a libertine and a rake."

"He is a poor dupe," she replied, and ate on, unperturbed.

She was loudly talked down by both gentlemen, till Maggie slipped in to support her view. Herbert, whatever of Allingcote, was too deep in the throes of infatuation to see their view. When he left the room without even touching the vast variety of splendid desserts collected, Clara assumed his passion had still a day or two to run its course.

"If Nel Muldoon lures Ormond into offering for her, Allingcote, I shall hold you entirely responsible," Clara warned him.

"He could do worse" was his unsatisfactory reply.

"No, he couldn't," Maggie said.

"With his pending title and her blunt, they'd make a good match," he insisted mulishly. "Nel is to be pitied in spite of all. She knows she hasn't been wanted for two years. By Anglin, by me, certainly by you and Mama, Maggie. She must know by now that even Moore was not after her *beaux yeux*, but her beau blunt. If she could feel someone liked her for herself, I think she might settle down."

"But would she be happy with a cretin?" Maggie asked.

Clara smiled, and Ben gave them a derisive look. "Jealous pair of witches. Leave me my illusions."

"She's young," Clara said. "In that our hope for her salvation must rest."

"You just want to get her off your hands without leaving her on your conscience," Maggie teased, knowing her brother pretty well.

"I'll have her off my hands tomorrow, and my conscience is clear. I've done my best for her for two years. I can't help it if I don't love her. The Bertrams have the reputation of being sensible people, and as they will be made aware of her history, I leave her in their hands. There is no reason she should not be presented next spring. She'd like that. In the interim, perhaps some respectable gent like Herbert will show her around town."

"Nel Muldoon will have gents wherever she goes," Maggie prophesied. "With her debut to look forward to, she may toe the line."

"She does care a little for her reputation," Clara said. "She didn't want people here to know what she'd been up to. With a larger audience to play to, she may even sink into propriety."

"I take credit for saving her fair name this time around," Maggie said. "I said Clara was tending her in her illness, but I couldn't think of any excuse for your absence, Ben."

"You lack Nel's power of invention. I have been running around the countryside looking for a doctor wonderful enough to save her life. We forgot to tell Herbert that, Clara."

"I'll do it," Maggie said, hopping up. "I daresay

you were just looking for an excuse to be rid of me, Ben. I don't mind in the least. I am contemplating falling in love with Mr. Ormond myself."

"You're taking your time about it," Ben smiled.

"Unlike some people, I haven't the knack of falling head over ears in love in three days," she said saucily, and left.

"One day, Maggie. One day," he called after her, and laughing, turned to Clara. "Do you believe in love at first sight, Clara?"

"Certainly. It is the only kind I do believe in. It is the vogue in all the best gothic novels. The eyes meet, an electric charge runs across the room, shattering the heart into smithereens."

He turned a lazy smile on her. "Something like that. But our eyes didn't meet, actually. You were looking at Boo Withers, standing close to the grate, holding your hands out to be warmed. The whelp grabbed hold of your hand and pulled you back. Do you know, that is when I first experienced the onset of these fits of violence that never go beyond the impulse. I wanted to push him right into the fire to be incinerated and soon figured out it was his grabbing you that caused it."

"You would have preferred to see my gown catch fire?"

"That would have been interesting, but I only wanted to grab you myself. I settled for detaching you from Withers instead. *Then* our eyes met, but my heart was already smashed to bits. No electric shock either, but a feeling of peace. I must not be reading the right novels."

"Mrs. Radcliffe would soon set you straight."

"I didn't need Mrs. Radcliffe to tell me I had met my doom. Er, make that destiny."

"I will make it your doom if I receive any more of these compliments, sir."

He cocked an ear and said, "There! Music to soothe the savage beast, right on cue." The plangent strains of violins and cellos began wafting through the house. It was only afternoon, but with the nuptial feast over, a dance was about to begin. Prissie and Oglethorpe were to lead off, before preparing for their departure for the Highlands.

Their hunger satisfied, Ben and Clara went to see the new baroness perform her first social duty. She did it with a noticeable lack of verve, but she was a lackluster girl at the best of times and was said to have performed handsomely. With a mama, a dresser, and a sister to get the bride into her traveling suit, Clara did think it a little hard that she must go abovestairs to help, too, but she alone knew the trick of tethering the silk scarf to the neck of the suit so that it didn't pop up at every step, and Prissie insisted that Clara help her.

When the bride was ready, there was a prolonged leave-taking. Lady Lucker cried real tears of joy to be creditably rid of her daughter at last. Sir James said, "Take care of her," in a brusque way to Oglethorpe. Prissie's groom failed to protect her from Maximilian's parting pinch, but he did bravely intrude his slender body between her and Nel Muldoon when Nel advanced to say her farewells.

There was a general exodus to the front door to see

the loaded traveling carriage begin its unenvied haul to Scotland. After the day's exertions, more food in the form of hot hors d'oeuvres was served. Lady Lucker foresaw no good use for them after her company had gone. Another hour passed before dancing resumed, and Allingcote appeared at Clara's side to claim her.

"Do we workers have to start collecting plates, or are we free to dance?" he asked, inclining his head to hers in his familiar way.

"I resign," Clara answered, stifling a yawn. "I haven't the energy for anything but falling over onto a sofa and going to sleep." Even as she spoke, a new wave of energy surged within her. She liked dancing, and particularly she looked forward to dancing with Ben.

"Dance with me," he insisted. "I'm dead on my feet, too. We may keel over in the middle of the floor, but we must have one dance to honor Prissie's wedding. We'll rest our weary bones till they play a waltz. I won't force the rollicking pace of a country-dance on you, but we must waltz."

Clara opened her mouth to say she was not actually so very tired. Ben misunderstood her intention and interrupted. "Don't be selfish, woman. Just because you haven't slept in three nights is no reason to refuse to dance for a couple of hours. You notice how subtly I shift the charge of selfishness on to your shoulders? One dance, then I'll let you have that sick headache you've been preparing since morning."

"Very well, as you are totally selfish and pig-headed, we'll have one waltz."

"Good girl. Wait right here." Ben went to speak to the musicians. A waltz struck up, but before he got back to her, she was asked to stand up with a different gentleman. She declined, politely at first, but the man was slightly the worse for wine, so that he insisted. Rather than cause a scene, she agreed to a dance.

When Ben returned to the spot where he had left her, he looked around in perplexity, then began scanning the floor till he found her. An expression of bewilderment was his first reaction; it soon firmed to annoyance. She looked at him with a helpless, apologetic gaze as his lips moved in mute profanity. Ben stood, arms akimbo, glaring for a moment, then strode onto the floor, and cut in on her partner. Her escort, pleasantly foxed, gave in with a good grace, and Allingcote swept Clara into his arms at last.

"Another strong compulsion to commit violence has been avoided—barely, and with no thanks to you," he said gruffly.

"I told him I had promised the dance. He insisted, and as he had been drinking, you know . . ."

"Never mind your excuses, my girl. I know well enough your custom of never remaining in one spot for ten seconds. It was my own fault. I should have dragged you with me to the orchestra. You would have enjoyed the little trip. This is going to be a very long dance, however, a whole guinea long, and I shouldn't begrudge the old souse a few seconds of it."

"Did you bribe them to play a waltz? What a shocking waste of money. They have been instructed to play several, included in their fee."

"Very likely, but what they were about to strike up was a cotillion. I wanted to have our waltz now. Well worth a guinea, too," he said warmly, pulling her more tightly against him.

"One would never take you for Lady Lucker's nephew. You have no economy."

"I fancy you have enough for both of us."

"Only when necessary—which is most of the time. What I would really like to do is get my hands on a fortune and buy every stupid thing I have always wanted. Gowns and bonnets and slippers . . ." She sighed in contemplation.

"A bit of a Nel Muldoon, in fact. Another of my little compliments for you."

Clara was too happy to revile him. She smiled and said in her usual calm way, "I expect it is fatigue making you so clumsy-tongued."

His arm, already holding her a shade tighter than was the custom, tightened with a jerk and his head loomed close above hers. His eyes glowed strangely bright. "I think I'm going to kiss you, Clara," he said in a husky voice. "Don't you think we should go somewhere more private?"

"What, and waste your guinea? No, no, like your primitive urges, it will soon pass away."

His feet stopped moving. He stood stock still in the middle of the floor, arousing some curiosity as waltzers jostled around them. "I don't think so. It seems to be getting stronger. If you don't want to scandalize Auntie's party still further, you had best come with me."

Before she had time to reply, Clara was waltzed

out the door and into the hallway. Ben opened the first door he came to. It led into a chamber that was surprisingly dark for afternoon. Lady Lucker never burned a lamp unless it was necessary, and the windows were heavily shrouded against the winter winds. When he closed the door behind them, it was black as a cave at midnight. Ben drew her against him, tightened his arms around her till she was reminded of his threat of forged steel chains, and kissed her long and passionately, in total silence. The darkness and silence added to the dreamlike quality of the moment. Obviously this was not happening. She had had too much wine and had dozed off into a delightful dream.

Then he raised his head. She felt his breaths against her cheek when he spoke. "I have been dreaming of this for two years. It is even better than I dreamed," he said, and kissed her again, with hungry, devouring kisses, while his arms crushed her to him. Clara thought she had been harboring some such dream all her grown-up life.

Their embrace was interrupted by a stertorous snort from the corner. "Oh!" Clara jumped in guilty surprise and pulled away.

Ben reached for her in the darkness, but his attempt to ignore the interruption was in vain. The snort changed to a querulous voice. "Who is there? Light the demmed lamps. Why are we plunged into darkness? Dashed skint."

Allingcote opened the door to let some weak light from the hall penetrate the room. It revealed Maximilian, sprawled on a sofa, just sitting up, and rubbing his head.

"Oh, it's you, Allingcote," he said. "Who are you cuddling there? Clara—*you*!" he exclaimed in shock. No amorous dealings surprised him for long, however, and he soon regained his composure. "Sly puss, letting on you didn't like it when I—Heh heh. I made sure it was the Muldoon. There is a girl I wouldn't mind— Well, well. I daresay you two would like to be alone. Try the next room, and be sure you close the door behind you when you leave," he said, and lay down again.

"An excellent idea. Sorry we disturbed you," Allingcote replied very civilly, and led Clara out, closing the door behind them. "Was that a feather pillow he was using, or his preferred kind? I didn't see a lady with him, did you?"

"We're disgraced!" Clara gasped. Her voice was pitched low, and her face was scarlet.

"He's drunk as a wheelbarrow; he won't remember a thing. You didn't tell me he has been at you with his pinches. Another victim for my violence list. I asked you to come in my carriage. Let it be a lesson to you. Now what did he say about another room . . ." He began looking down the hall.

"No! Have you no shame? I'm going back to the dance."

"As well hang for a sheep as a lamb." With a tight hold on her hand, he headed to another room, but Clara was adamant.

"I am not going in there with you, Ben."

"Clara, we're *two years* overdue for this." His voice

197

trembled with emotion. She clenched her lips and shook her head. "Oh very well. We might catch a few shillings of that guinea I wasted." He allowed himself to be dragged back to the dance floor, to finish the long waltz, and then lay plans for the morrow.

A discussion with Lady Lucker revealed that her family and Clara would go to London the day following the next. Ben made some halfhearted hints that he could stay over the extra day and take Nel to London on the later day. An unencouraging silence from his aunt prompted him to follow his original course and leave the next day. He then sought out his mother and Maggie and coerced them into going to London with him. Clara was unclear why he should do this, when it had been their intention to return directly to Braemore. They offered no objection, however, and it was settled with many sly smiles from Maggie's direction.

It was also arranged that Ben would call on his aunt and Clara in London the day they arrived. By repeated hints he talked Lady Lucker into leaving in the morning, not much after ten, which would get her to London in early afternoon. She had planned to arrive only in time for dinner, thus giving herself time to get her own house in order before leaving. When all the details were hammered out to Allingcote's last whim, the gathering disbanded, and he turned to Clara.

"It is perfectly understood now that I go to London tomorrow, unload Nel, and call on you the next afternoon around three at Percy Lucker's house in Belgrave Square. You won't have any little surprises for me?"

"It is all arranged. I'll be there."

"If you let me down, tumbleweed, I'll come after you, and all my empty threats of violence will be executed. Fur will fly. Possibly also bullets and knives and—*be* there!"

"I'll be there, I promise."

He directed a worried, ardent gaze on her, and as he gazed, the frown faded from his face. "Very well. I consider that a vow. And now at last you can go to bed and have that headache you've been rehearsing all day. I'll get the leash on Nel and see she doesn't make a bolt for the border with Herbert. Will you be up to see us off tomorrow?"

"What time do you plan to leave?"

"Not early. London's only three hours away. In fact, I'll stick around till afternoon if Aunt Charity doesn't show me the door sooner."

"I'll see you before you go then. I never sleep till noon."

"We'll try and see if we can rout Max out of our room." A soft smile entered his eyes and lifted the corners of his lips.

They were standing in the hall, and when he began looking toward that room with a certain light in his eyes, Clara thought it sad but wise to escape while she could. She ran up the stairs. When she got to the top, she turned and saw Ben gazing up after her, smiling bemusedly, like a man in a trance.

She was in a trancelike state herself as she undressed for bed. She was sleeping in Prissie's room that night, the only chamber yet vacated. The bridal gown hung on the wall, giving rise to delightful thoughts of the future. She held it before her and looked in the mirror. She looked like a young girl again, a young girl very much in love.

Chapter Seventeen

Worn to the socket, Clara slept late the next morning. At ten forty-five she first opened her eyes to look about the strange room in which she slept, with the white bridal gown hanging on the wall. Whatever she had been dreaming, she had for a moment the awful feeling that she had been married and missed her own wedding. As memories washed over her, she laughed a soft, gurgling sound and bounded out of bed.

She was so happy that a song formed on her lips and she hummed as she tidied the bed. Ninnyhammer, she smiled to herself. No one has asked you to be his wife yet. But he had as well as asked, and the tumultuous joy in her breast was the response. She proceeded to make a toilette worthy of this day of days, knowing it would be subjected to a lover's close scrutiny.

Her mirror told her the ravages of fatigue had been dissipated by her long rest. Her cheeks were rosy, her eyes sparkling, and soon her curls were neatly brushed into their customary bun. Her gold gown that became her well, in spite of its long service, was enhanced with her late mother's pearls; and with a luxurious sigh of sheer pleasure, Clara went tripping downstairs. All her pains were for nought. Nel had arisen at nine, after staying up till one o'clock. She had decreed that she wished to leave for London at once, probably because Herbert Ormond had already left. Allingcote put her off till ten-thirty, then he ran out of excuses and gave in to Nel's insistence.

"Ben said you would know what the plans are in any case," Lady Lucker said vaguely. Clara deduced that Ben had not told his aunt of the attachment between them and kept her silence on that score. "Now we have a great deal to do, Clara. I would like to get all the dishes returned before we leave for London—all that are empty, for there are several not even touched. The roasts will keep till we return, and the cakes and what not. I shall take Mrs. Frieman's dressed partridge with us for Uncle Percy. One dislikes to land in empty-handed. The petits fours will come in handy in London as well, but we can put them in a tin and return the plates."

A lengthy discussion of this domestic nature followed, and before they parted to begin their duties, the post arrived.

"From London," Lady Lucker exclaimed, glancing at the envelope. "Fortunately it is franked. It must be from Percy. He is about the only one who did not come to the wedding, but at his age—"

"Perhaps it is from Charles," Clara said.

"No, it is not in his hand. I wonder what it can be. A belated message to Prissie, no doubt."

With no premonition of any more serious message than that, Clara watched while Lady Lucker perused her note. Her hostess was neither smiling nor frowning as she put the note aside. "Uncle Percy has a dreadful case of influenza, and the trip to London must be put off," she announced. Clara blinked dumbly, as if she had just been told the world was coming to an end.

"Truth to tell, I am half relieved," Lady Lucker confided, thinking the forlorn face of her guest was on her hostess's behalf. "The trip has served its purpose in getting rid of the others, who would otherwise hang about for weeks, you know. We have the house full of good food, and I really do not relish the trip in the cold. We shall not mention to the others that the trip is canceled. As soon as they leave, we can settle in as cozy as bugs in a rug and relax, after the strains of the wedding."

It was foolish to feel the world was ending, only because of a little delay. But Clara could not suppress the sensation that an Arctic cloud had swept over Branelea, robbing her day of the promised sunshine. "But—but your sister, Lady Allingcote, is expecting you," she said.

"Peg won't be staying above a day or two herself. It was all Ben's idea. He is never happy unless he is jauntering about somewhere or other. He has scarcely been at Braemore more than a month at a stretch since his papa's death."

Knowing now the reason for his jauntering, Clara

made another effort to get her hostess off to London. "You could stay with Lady Allingcote. There is really no need to put off the trip only because Percy Lucker is unwell. Indeed, I imagine you would like to just drop by and see him, to help him if you could."

"I wouldn't go near him with a barge pole while he is infected. I daresay the whole of London is rife with flu. We are better off where we are. I cannot think what Peg is about, going there in the dead of winter."

"You will notify her at least?" Clara asked, wondering if she could include a note to Allingcote in the missive.

"She will hear it from Percy's servants. Ben is to drop by tomorrow, you recall, so there is no need to write. She will know it before the letter could reach her."

"That is true," Clara admitted, searching her mind for further bait.

"Well, I wonder how Prissie and Oglethorpe are making out," the mother said, bringing the discussion of London to a close.

It was not so easily forgotten by Clara. What would Ben say when she once again failed to be where she was supposed to be—had promised, in fact had practically vowed, she would be? As she worked, she canvased a dozen schemes of getting to London by herself, every one of them highly ineligible. Sir James was no ally; he would sooner be in his study with his collection than in heaven. There were half-a-dozen coaches leaving for London that very day, but Lady Lucker had loaded her down with chores.

She could not blithely announce she was leaving. In fact a mantle of secrecy cloaked the fact that Lady Lucker was not going to London, lest any of the guests decided to prolong their visit. For Clara to beg a drive in another carriage would be bound to raise suspicions.

And where could she stay if she did wedge her way into a coach? Sir Percy was ill. The Allingcotes had not invited her to go to them. She hadn't enough money for a hotel, or any companion to lend her respectability. It would look so excessively odd in any case for her to dash off to London alone to stay in a hotel. It would cast a doubt on Lady Lucker's hospitality. No, it was impossible. She had not been in touch with any of her London friends or relatives lately. At the festive season they might very well be away visiting. There was Herbert—left that very morning! But a bachelor living in an apartment was of no use to her. She even thought of the Bertrams, Nel's relatives. When she realized how far into the realms of fancy she had strayed, she called herself back to reality.

She was not going to London. She was staying at Branelea, and the only hope for the future was that Ben would learn, as soon as he went to Percy's, that she was still at Branelea. It was unfortunate in the extreme, but it was unavoidable. She cheered herself with the thought that Lady Allingcote might invite her to join them in London, or possibly even at Braemore—that had been mentioned earlier. There were guests leaving throughout the day, to keep things lively. Every time a coach left for London,

Clara had to restrain the urge to throw herself into it. She would stand at the door, blinking back an unshed tear, as it bowled down the drive to begin its way to London.

In London, Ben delivered Nel Muldoon to the Bertrams, whom he was happy to see were good, sensible people. He stayed for some time talking to them and was impressed with their fitness for the job they were undertaking. They were by no means Quakerishly strict; they spoke of parties and plays. Soon Nel and Mrs. Bertram were discussing gowns and modistes in a friendly manner. Ben considered it a blessing that Mrs. Bertram was pretty herself. He persisted in his notion that a pretty lady would be less likely to take Nel in dislike. There was also enough difference in their ages that they would not be competing for the same beaux.

When the chaperon was heard to say, "I always wanted a daughter—but I wager she would not have been half as pretty as you," Ben breathed a sigh of relief. He had little doubt that by nightfall Nel would be calling Mrs. Bertram "Mama," for she was always happy to assume a new role. He met Herbert Ormond going up the walk as he came out. They met now as old friends. Really Ben liked him amazingly, all of a sudden.

He drove to his own house and dashed off a line to assure Anglin that his charge was delivered into safe hands. He then set the servants bustling about polishing and cleaning and cooking. All unaware of Sir Percy's indisposition, Ben's day was much happier than Clara's. The next morning he was up bright and early. He had to visit his man of business, had to send to Braemon for more servants, and pay a visit to Dunn's caterers to discuss a wedding breakfast. He would hire a French chef for their sojourn in London, and a good French chef was not hired in a week. Every fifteen minutes he glanced at his watch, to see how soon he might call at Belgrave Square.

He was at Sir Percy's door at three on the dot, to be confronted by the butler with the news that the company from Branelea was not coming after all. Sir Percy was unwell—the doctor was with him at that very moment. "But Miss Christopher is here," Ben said. The butler's doubting frown told him she had foiled him again.

"Ah, Miss Christopher. That would be Lady Lucker's houseguest? No, milord, none of the party from Branelea has come."

"You're sure she's not coming?"

"No one from Branelea is expected, sir."

There was no point in further protestations. The butler already took him for a fool. "I might have known," Ben said fatalistically, and walked away without another word, or any thought of violence at all. He returned to his own house and spoke to his mother.

"I am leaving for Branelea at once, Mama," he said, and explained his reason.

"What a pity. It's getting late, dear. Why do you not wait and go tomorrow? Why, she might come tomorrow herself, with one of Charity's guests. That Mr. Ormond—"

"Mr. Ormond is already here. She's not coming. I can be there not long after dark if I leave at once. I'll have her here by midday tomorrow. Is her room ready?"

"Yes, Ben, everything is ready. We have given her the blue suite, and there are plenty of logs by the grate, and even flowers. Maggie bought some from a street peddler. But I wonder why Miss Christopher did not come with some of the others. Why, Maximilian traveled alone, as far as I know."

"Ah well," he said resignedly. "She would not want to come with him. She bruises easily."

"So do I!" his mother said, rubbing her hip. "I shall warn Charity another time not to place him within arm's length of me."

"You should have worn your corsets, Mama," Maggie quizzed. "Would you like me to go with you for company, Ben?"

"I would like your company to go, but then you would be in the carriage for the return trip as well, and three, you know, is a crowd," he replied frankly.

"You see how it will be once he is shackled, Mama!"

"I have some hope that from now on, Ben won't be living in his carriage," his mother laughed.

It was four when Ben left. The falling darkness slowed his journey, and he did not arrive till eight. At Branelea, meals had returned to their regular country hours. By eight Clara and Lady Lucker were sitting before the grate in the gold saloon, mending their stockings while Sir James sorted his Roman coins at a table on the side. They all looked to the doorway when they heard the knocker sound. "Someone has lost a wheel or lamed a nag, and has come back to find a night's free lodging," Lady Lucker scolded.

Clara said nothing, but her face turned pale, and her heart beat fiercely in her breast. Within seconds Ben loomed in the doorway, still wearing his great coat and holding his curled beaver in his hand. He directed one long, hard stare at Clara before turning to his aunt.

"You've never brought that girl back here!" was Lady Lucker's chilly welcome.

"Nel is with the Bertrams in London," he answered. Halfway through the sentence he turned to glare again at Clara.

"Why are you here then?" his aunt asked, alive with curiosity.

"Mama asked me to see if Miss Christopher would come to us for a visit."

Clara was surprised and elated that he had come so soon. He must have left the minute he heard from Percy that she was not coming to London. Such eagerness for her company was, of course, highly flattering, but she realized full well she would have to account for her not being there. The dark looks directed on her by the caller left her in no doubt on that score.

"I cannot part with Clara just yet," Lady Lucker said. "Peg spoke to me about having her at Braemore later, but with Prissie gone and winter stretching drearily before us, I cannot like to part with her just yet."

"I am afraid you must, Auntie," he said in a voice that brooked no denial. He turned to Clara again and directed one final scorching look at her.

Charity Lucker was the sharpest woman in the parish, but from having her mind totally occupied with the intricacies of Prissie's wedding, she had failed to notice that Ben was in love with Clara. It was not slow in coming to her that she had missed out on an occurrence of major importance. Once she realized it, she acted with the greatest promptitude, for she had grown peculiarly fond of Clara Christopher and thought she would make Ben a wonderful, economical wife. Her way of stretching a penny would more than make up for her lack of a dowry in the long haul. She could not have been happier if Clara had been a great heiress.

"In that case, I daresay you two have a dozen plans to make," she smiled, and rose. "James, dear, will you just come along with me a moment," she began, trying to give the lovers privacy.

"Eh? What's that?" he asked, peering over the top of his spectacles.

"I want to speak to you, dear."

"Yes, yes. In a moment. I think I have got a rare coin here. See the date—" He took up his magnifying glass to read numbers into an accumulation of rust and mud. He remained unmovable, and with a swift shift of plans, Lady Lucker turned to Ben. "Why do you two not go into the study? There is a fire lit, for James usually plays with his coins in there." A fire lit in an unused chamber required an excuse, to her own conscience if no one else.

"Excellent," Ben said. He tossed his hat aside, took off his coat, and put out his hand to Clara. With no more signs of all her discomposure than a shy smile and a color a little heightened, Clara went with him to stand before an extremely meager fire in the study grate.

Ben turned to face her, a spark kindling his eyes. "Explain yourself, young lady," he said in a strained voice.

"I—I assumed you had an explanation from Percy's house, in London. He is ill you see, and so of course our trip was put off."

"And of course you could not have come to *me*! Clara, you *promised faithfully*."

"I had no way of getting there."

"There must have been dozens of carriages making the trip from Branelea to London today."

She forbore going into the intricacies of not announcing to the guests that Lady Lucker's trip was off and said instead, "But where could I stay? I could not go barging into your house uninvited. I had no idea whether you would have room . . ."

"Aunt Charity knows very well we have fourteen bedrooms! Not even a line or a word to let me know."

"There was no time. And it would be improper to write to you when we are not engaged or anything."

He looked as if she had struck him. "Not engaged?" he asked, astonished. "Clara, we are practically married! I have already ordered the wedding dinner. What have I been doing the past days if not proposing my head off? You haven't shown any aversion to the idea. Really this caution goes beyond understanding. It is inexcusable. You should be—I don't know what is *bad* enough for you. You should be dunked like a common scold, in a cold pond in December."

Warmed by his angry love, she said in a teasing way, "Or have both my legs broken?"

"It would keep you in one place at least."

"But I have stayed in one place, and you don't like that either," she pouted.

"It was the wrong place. I wanted you *there*, with *me*."

"Well, I am here with you now," she pointed out.

"You shouldn't be. Not engaged!" he said, shaking his head in disbelief. "Clara, really—what did you mean by leading me on in the parlor in front of Maximilian if you don't consider yourself engaged?"

"I was not leading you on! You leapt at me—and you never breathed a syllable about marriage either."

"I suppose till I go down on my bended knee and tell you I love you half-a-dozen times you won't realize that rather obvious fact either."

"Very true. You come to know me uncommonly well. A lady dare not admit she's smitten till she gets her offer," she replied, refusing to be cowed by his temper.

"I love you. I love you. I love you. *I love you*," he repeated again and again, his voice rising with anger and impatience. "Dammit, I have loved you forever, Clara, as you know very well."

"That's five," she said, ticking them off on her fingers.

"I love you. That's six," he said, advancing toward her with a menacing scowl.

"I am glad to hear it, because you look as if you mean to murder me," she said, retreating toward the grate as he advanced.

"Don't you have something to add to that—five or six times?"

"Well, I suppose I love you, too," she said uncertainly.

"Not good enough, miss!" His hands rose as he leaned toward her.

"All right! I love you!" she shrieked, jumping back as if in fright. "Oh dear, I am not at all sure I want to marry a savage ape!" she said, laughing.

"Tame me then," he said softly. Already a tamer air hung around him, and a tender light glowed in his eyes. "Stroke me. Speak softly to me. Tell me how much you love me." He reached out a hand that did not seem bent on violence and possessed himself of her fingers, which he squeezed ever so gently.

"I'll remind you in ten years, if you haven't returned to the jungle or been locked up with the other wild beasts at the Tower."

"I'll be around. You will regret that rash promise, my cautious Clara. But for the time being, let us just back up a decade and get our marriage settled. We *are* getting married, Clara. You mentioned January as being a good month."

"I said December."

"We have less than four hours," he said, looking at the mantle clock. "This is the thirty-first. We'll have to do it here. I thought London . . ."

She began to smile, till she realized he was serious. A contemplative frown had seized his face. "Ben, you're mad! I'm not ready—we couldn't possibly—"

"January then. It's even duller than December, and I know Mama and Maggie are looking forward to being there for the exchange of vows."

"Next year—"

"Dear girl, if you mean next December, it is you who are mad. I don't plan to wait another twelve months!"

"A spring wedding would be lovely."

"Charming, but the spring, you told me, has its own pleasures, and how are we to get on in the dull winter months?"

"What a lack of imagination. There are sleigh rides and skating."

"And this." He pulled her roughly into his arms, and kissed her so hard and so long that it seemed a few weeks at least of the winter might slip by with less dullness than feared.

Disengaging herself, Clara began to say in a distracted way, "We could always . . ." She had some unclear thought of saying they could go at once to London to get married.

"Yes, darling, a dozen other delightful diversions occur to me, too, but we really should be married first, you know." From the furious manner in which he went on to divert himself, Clara, cautious still, was strongly inclined to agree with him.

With a last burst of conscience, she tried to persuade him to rejoin the Luckers in the gold saloon. He professed admiration for the few embers moldering in the grate, and with an eye on the comfortable armchair, thought it would hold two very nicely, being designed for one. It took the bribe of an uncut glass of claret and considerable struggling to get him into the gold saloon, and even then he went reluctantly.

"Well, my dear, when do you plan to leave?" Lady Lucker asked eagerly as soon as they came in.

"Pushing me out again, Auntie?" Ben asked with a good-natured smile, the savage lulled. "Take care or we won't ask you to our wedding."

"Ben! Is it indeed to be a match? I couldn't be happier. James, do you hear this?" She went to Clara and embraced her.

"Very nice. Very nice indeed," Sir James said. "Congratulations and all that. Ben, you were at the Roman Museum the other day. Tell me if you saw anything like this." He held a coin out to him, but Ben could not recall seeing its match elsewhere. He scarcely saw the one held under his nose.

"You have got yourself a very able manager here, Ben," Lady Lucker said, ignoring her husband entirely. "My own girls could not run a house better. Not half so well. Clara will have your household in order in no time, and not cost you a fortune to do it either. When do you mean to get married?"

Clara had tentatively in mind a short holiday in London, with perhaps a remove to Braemore and a wedding there in a month.

"Next week," Ben said.

"A small do then," she nodded. "Very wise. After just being through a large one, I must commend your wisdom. Though you must be sure to send all your relatives notices, Clara. There is no reason you must be diddled out of your gifts, only because you are having a small do."

"I doubt it can be arranged in a week, Ben," Clara said.

"It can. We'll get a licence immediately when we get to London. Mama and Maggie have things well in hand. Ordering plenty of glasses and so on," he said, with a brief but speaking glance to Clara.

"There is no need to *buy* them, Ben," his aunt objected at once. "Take what you need from here and return them on your way to Braemore."

"We won't be returning to Braemore till the spring. Mama and Maggie will, I expect, but Clara and I have decided to honeymoon in London."

"Not a bad idea. It will save traveling expenses and having to put up at expensive hotels."

"Exactly," Ben agreed with unsteady lips. "And Clara needs to do such a lot of shopping that we will be watching every penny," he continued unblushing. "Gowns, bonnets, slippers—was that not what you said, Clara?"

Clara said not a word, but cast a look of revulsion on her outspoken groom. Lady Lucker nodded her agreement. "Clara knows just where to buy wisely." Visions of the Pantheon Bazaar rose in her mind's eye.

"Mama wants you and Sir James to come to us as soon as you conveniently can," Ben said.

"We will be there in a day or two," Lady Lucker promised. "Oh and Clara, there are dozens of things left over from Prissie's wedding—half of that huge ham and sweets and so on. I shall take a box of them with me."

"You are very kind, Aunt Charity," Ben said, "but we really don't want to have a wedding breakfast of leftovers. For that one occasion, we are going to splurge."

His aunt looked doubtful at this poor beginning, but placed enough faith in Clara's good sense that she had no real fear of improvidence on this scale continuing.

"This calls for a celebration," Sir James said. The racket going forth prevented him from doing justice to his bent and discolored coins. "A glass of champagne, what?"

Lady Lucker prepared to intervene with the mention that Ben preferred claret. But there was champagne left over from the wedding, and she decided to splurge with this last magnanimous gesture.

The toast was drunk, and with no more nonsense, James was led from the room. Lady Lucker dashed off to the parlor where Prissie's gifts were laid out, to run her eye over the lot for duplicates and determine what she could part with for Clara's gift. Ben's silver tea service and the Wedgwood cups were tallied up with Clara's wineglasses, and the decision taken that Prissie had no possible use for an ugly silver epergne featuring naked nymphs and some strange man with wings on his heels.

"What will your mother say to rushing things forward so?" Clara asked Ben.

"She will say, 'Hallelujah and amen.' She has not

liked to see me racketing around the countryside, looking for you. It was her idea to stay in London and oversee things. She hasn't Charity's knack for cutting a corner, so it will be your lot to see she won't go buying the food herself, instead of dunning the neighbors for it."

"A pity I am not acquainted with your neighbors."

"The caterer will provide us a fresh feast with no bother at all."

"Ben, you're talking about pounds and pounds—of money, I mean."

"You will be in charge of curbing my wild extravagance, as well as my ferocity."

"A week doesn't give me much time to do either."

"It offers too many opportunities—seven whole days—for you to vanish on me. Maggie and Mama will go with you to see to your trousseau, if you like. Whatever you can get made up in a week. The rest of the time you will be with me, tied leg and wing."

With a guinea left of her allowance, Clara foresaw the need for some considerable skill in assembling a creditable trousseau. With the most careful of contriving, she did not see how it could be done at less than five.

"Not to worry, Clara," Ben said, smiling at her fondly. "I mean to keep you quite as busy as Aunt Charity did, but I shall pay you better. I am arranging a settlement with my man of business."

"Oh I—I have some money," she said in embarrassment.

"Yes, love, I know you have a guinea and seven shillings, unless you've been squandering it on shoelaces and headache powders, but I am talking about an allowance. Don't blush, Clara. We're getting married. It is the custom, you know, for a husband to support his wife."

"It's not the custom for a lord to marry someone so poor as I am," she pointed out calmly.

"You contradict yourself. You told me it was all the crack for a wealthy lord to marry a penniless beauty. I daresay you were dropping me a hint then, but I was too dense to see it."

"Don't remind me of all the stupid things I said."

"I won't. But in ten years' time, I'll remind you of one of your brighter remarks. And now I remind you of your primary duty. I am beginning to feel savage, Clara. Do something about it," he demanded.

She poured him another glass of champagne. He set it aside with a heavy frown and advanced toward her in a stalking fashion.

Regency presents the popular and prolific...
JOAN SMITH